KIMA BLAZE

A Cursed Legacy

A RIFT IN THE VEIL book 3

To my Writing Community

Contents

The residents of the Spirit World cannot stay there. The land needs time to heal, and so it can't have creatures feeding off of it. They all know, and they have all agreed to leave it for the time it needs. Some even know how to speed the healing along and will do so. But to do so involves travel. They must go past the Grey World that has kept them safe, and travel to the World of Man to bring back more energy for the Spirit World to feed on. They will do so.

However, some spirits want the powers of the World of Man for themselves. They want to use it to grow strong, like in the legends of old. To become what they were always meant to be, if not for the mutts meddling. It is time for the spirits to have their revenge, and no mutt can stop them.

So the Spirit World is empty, and the Grey World is full. Creatures big and small traveling through. Some with plans to return to help their own world. Some with hopes of a better life in this unknown World of Man. Some wishing to take what they have always thought their right.

And the World of Man has no idea what's coming.

1

Someone is sitting on my chest. A woman is straddling me and leaning over me, her hair slipping into my mouth and down my throat... Drowning. Water filling my mouth and... mom's hands around my throat, squeezing... tick, tock, tick, tock, tick, to... My darling holding my hand as we hung upside down in the car, his face the last... Fire licking our flesh, eating us, like...The woman was smiling with no mouth... too much noise, too many harmful things...tick, tock, tick, tock... moving through a world of fog, we were alone. We were always together, but not here, not... Blood was trickling down my face from my mouth, blinding me. All the blood... Every time, every world, has graveyards; this one's weren't hard to find, now just to wait... tick, tock, tick... Connor's eyes weren't his anymore as the wendigo took him over... Gasping for breath as the earth packed itself around me... tick, tock... aunt Ellie was floating in the water... dancing through the fall-dormant trees without moving, singing with the voice of the leaves... Feeding off their nightmares... tick... smashing in the boy's head with a rock... tock... I was dying!

The mattress moved under me, and I woke. Somewhere, a rocking chair was moving back and forth, and the singsong voice of children slipped through the closed door. At the end of the bed, Sara put my phone down on the bedside table.

"What time is it?" I asked, voice groggy.

She jumped. "Holy stars, I thought you were asleep."

I sat up and grimaced. My ribs hurt. "No. Or, I was, but not anymore. Why did you move?"

"Your alarm woke me."

I yawned and carefully pulled the duvet up around my shoulders. She moved across the bed and buried under it with me, her hands cold against my warm skin. I gasped and shuddered, and she giggled in response. She rested her head on my shoulder, and together we leaned back against the wall. It felt like my whole back was one big bruise.

"Wanna go back to sleep?" Sara asked after a while.

"No."

"The dreams?"

"Yes, but most of them weren't the creature, I think."

"Oh?"

"Yes. I dreamed both of aunt Ellie's deaths." My voice cracked at the words, and I cleared my throat and closed my eyes to hide the tears forming there. "And there were the fires that got Elizabeth and the twins. And mom when she... on that night. And Connor last night." My voice trailed off for a moment as all these horrible events moved through my mind. Sara was moving her fingers in slow circles against my naked arms, trying to keep me calm, I guess. It gave me something to focus on, if nothing else. "And there were other memories."

"Memories?"

"I think the dying memories of all the ghosts downstairs."

A heavy hush fell between us. I was sure she could hear the rocking chair, but not the voices now giggling, and the little feet running down the stairs.

"They're still here?" Sara finally asked.

"I think so."

Another hush. I didn't know about Sara, but I was thinking about what needed doing. About all the ghosts that were downstairs and wanted my help to move on, wherever they were going. About the fact that I didn't know how to do it, despite having sent aunt Ellie on. I had no idea if she was where she was supposed to be or if I'd ruined her soul by using my necromancy on her. Then there was Connor, my father. He'd been taken over by a wendigo that had been drawn to my fright of ghosts for the energy they stored. The wendigo wanted to eat them until it was strong enough to take over a human. Thanks to me, all the ghosts in Sky Harbour were outside and ripe for the taking, which led to Connor being possessed. Then there were the dreams. The creatures moving through the forest. The woman sitting on my chest so I couldn't breathe. The things hunting in the night.

Somewhere in the house, someone laughed so loud it made my ears hurt. I buried my face in Sara's green hair for a moment before I pushed away from her and started looking for my clothes.

"What're you doing?" Sara asked as she moved to the edge of the bed, resting her naked feet on the floor.

"I'm not going back to sleep, so might as well do something smart with the time,"

I answered, trying to pull on a sweater without lifting my arms.

With a sigh, Sara stood and helped me. "Like what?"

I groaned and struggled until the sweater was in place. For a moment, I felt naked without a bra, but it would hurt my bruised torso, so better not. "I had an idea yesterday."

Sara pulled up her jeans, looking at me expectantly.

"I'm having nightmares of things that are really out there, right?" I said

"Yeah?"

"Why were dreamcatchers a thing to begin with? Maybe to catch these things that move in the dark and give me nightmares." Sara didn't say anything, just motioned for me to sit on the bed so she could help me with my socks. I let her boss me around but continued talking. "And I have one hanging in my bedroom at home, so why not go and get it?"

She stopped arguing with my sock and looked up, her eyes shining in the weak light coming through the window. "Want me to do it?"

Something coiled in my stomach and wanted to push up my throat, but I swallowed it. "No. It's time I go home."

"If you say so." She stood and held out her hand to me. I took it and let her pull me to my feet. "But I'm not letting you go alone. Wanna go right now? Before the others're up?" I nodded, not sure I'd answer correctly if I opened my mouth. "Let's go, then."

She pulled me across the bedroom and opened the door.

The rocker and voices quieted down.

2

We hadn't even set foot on the stairs before the first ghost appeared. He shot up through the floor right in front of me, and I stepped through him before I'd even registered what was going on.

"In my day –" he began, and I swear his voice came from inside my stomach. I gave a soft shriek and hurried forward, dragging Sara down the stairs.

"What just happened?" she asked, almost stumbling in my haste, but I hardly heard her over the angry woman now by my side.

"You said you were gonna help us," she said, voice almost roaring in my ear.

"Why won't you help?" A young boy asked from where he stood on the landing. As we rushed toward him, he stumbled back against the wall and fell right through it.

"Young woman," another man said, trying to block my way down the steps.

Behind him, filling the ground floor of the house and blocking the stairs, stood ghosts of and from every age. All of them were begging for my attention, trying to talk louder than the ghost beside them. In between them, my own spirits were moving around, trying to calm the others or make them shut up.

I let Sara's hand go and covered my ears.

Sara moved to stand in front of me, her brow furrowed. Above the hum of voices and the rush of my own body, I heard her ask if I was ok. I shook my head and formed the word ''ghosts'' with my mouth. Her furrow turned from worry to annoyance, and she turned around, looking over the sea of people without seeing them. I couldn't guess what she was saying as I couldn't see her lips, but whatever it was, it made the ghosts stop talking. When she was done, she turned, took one of my hands and pulled me down the rest of the stairs. The ghosts parted around her, but I still kept a wary eye on them as we put on our jackets and shoes.

Outside, the air was cold and crisp. Frost covered the ground and surfaces around us, our breath came out in small, white clouds, and the world smelled of smoke and snow. It was dark, and the clouds that had started forming in the east the night before now covered the entire sky.

"What did you say to them?" I asked as we walked down the porch steps.

"Just this and that," Sara said, smiling.

"She said she would put a *le fléau* on them all if they did not give you some space, Ms. Lizzie," Eleanor said.

I jumped at the sudden presence of my ghosts. Sara, just ahead of me, didn't notice when I turned to look at the group.

Eleanor was blond and dressed in a white cotton nightgown that billowed weakly around her naked legs. One of her pretty, pale hands rested on her swollen, pregnant belly, and the other held the hand of little Magdalena, six years old and in her own nightgown and wool stockings, her hair made out in golden ringlets around her shoulders. Just behind them, fourteen-year-old Elizabeth was walking, dressed in a puffy creation of pink fabric and yellow lace. She kept an eye on her younger siblings, the nine-year-old twins Jonathan and Johana, dressed in a matching set of blue outfits. They'd died in 1743, 1899, and 1851 respectably.

Looking at them like this, sorrow and guilt stabbed at my stomach. Two ghosts were missing—Sanderson and my aunt Ellie. We'd lost them less than forty-eight hours ago. I forgot to breathe for a moment, but not long enough for Sara to notice.

We were in the middle of the road now, walking straight for my childhood home. It loomed over us, a three-and-a-half story Queen Anne's surrounded by smaller but no less old Victorian homes. While there were lights on in the other houses, mine was dark and empty, seeming foreboding. The fear I felt for what had happened there froze out all the other feelings coiling within me, and for a brief moment, I considered running in the other direction.

"Did you really say you would curse the ghosts?" I asked Sara, walking a little faster to catch up to her. I hoped talking would distract me enough to do this.

She glanced at me, then around. "They told you?" I nodded, and she shrugged. "Well, yeah. Need to learn respect, you know? So far, you're the only one that can help 'em."

"Not if I don't know how to help, no."

"We'll figure something out. Maybe your mom knew?"

We were on the curb now, and I gripped the iron gate and looked up at the old Victorian mansion. My family home. Both Sanderson and Magdalena had been born in this house, but only Magdalena had died there. Or, not quite. Both mom and I had died here as well. I wasn't sure I could count myself, however, as I had come back. I suppressed a shudder.

"Mom's dead," I said and pushed the gate open. It squealed

and I cringed, afraid I'd wake the rest of the neighborhood.

"So? Not like that means nothing to you," Sara closed the gate behind her.

"If she's hanging around, don't you think I would have seen her by now?"

"Do everyone hang around?"

I stopped and looked to my ghosts, but they shrugged. Or, Elizabeth and the twins shrugged. Eleanor made some weird tilt with her head, and Magdalena shook her head in that way only a six-year-old can.

"I don't know," I answered and started up the porch steps.

Reaching the door, I stopped and took a deep breath. I'd only been back once after... that night, and I hadn't been able to stay for longer than a few minutes. The memories were too real for me, because I was able to see them play out again and again, like a TikTok-clip. Would they be gone by now, or would I have to see mom killing me all over again?

Drawing another deep breath, I grabbed for the keys.

It felt like the whole world was waiting for me as I unlocked and opened the door.

The house hadn't been empty for long, but it felt abandoned and hostile. Almost like it was angry with me for not staying home the day before yesterday. Could a house have feelings?

I kicked off my unlaced all-stars and walked deeper into the house, turning on lights as I went. At the bottom of the stairs, I looked up at the landing and waited for the memory of Mark to crash into the old grandfather clock to appear. Just when I was hoping he wouldn't come, he tumbled down. I suppressed a shiver and headed up the stairs, Sara and the ghosts close behind.

"Do you really think mom knew anything about ghosts?" I

asked Sara in a low voice as we made our way past mom and Connor's old room and up the next set of stairs. It felt like the house was listening, and I didn't like it.

"Maybe? Grams did say Nancy drove all the spirits away from the neighborhood somehow. Maybe she helped 'em move on?"

"But Mrs. Hearth also said she thought mom didn't really know how she did it."

Sara shrugged. "Maybe she knew more than she thought she knew?"

I glanced at her before entering my bedroom. This room felt less stuffy than the others in the house, but I still hurried. I tried reaching for the dreamcatcher, but my ribs screamed their protest, and I curled into a ball, grunting in pain. Glancing over my shoulder, I saw that Sara was nowhere in sight. I could ask her to get it, but I really didn't want to. Instead, I hurried into my closet, found one of my umbrellas, and hurried out again. I used the point at the end of the umbrella to slip the string off the nail from above the window.

Grabbing the dreamcatcher, I lay the umbrella down on the bed, muttering a happy ''thank you'' as I did. The thought that I was actually thanking the umbrella made me smile humorlessly. Did things have souls? I didn't know, but my world had gotten a lot bigger over the last week, so better safe than sorry.

Clutching the dreamcatcher, I left the bedroom, turning off the light as I went.

Sara was sitting on the sofa by the huge window looking over the garden. I stood behind her for a moment, taking in the view. The garden had once looked beautiful, but it was overgrown and unkempt now. A tall fence of brick ran to the right and left for almost a hundred meters before stopping with another high wall. The wall was overgrown with ivy and climbing roses long since asleep for the winter. A patch was set aside to grow berry bushes and the like, and they'd run wild, escaping their small patch and spreading over the grounds. There was a gazebo that really needed a new layer of paint, and an old treehouse that was probably a death trap if any kid should find their way into it. Trees stood huge and mature within the garden, the source of all the leaves on the ground, and even older trees leaned over the back fence, trying to reclaim what had once been forest. Hidden from view because of the angle and the roof of the small veranda below, was the dark spot where Sanderson had died.

The thought of it shook me out of my reverie. "Let's go," I said and turned away.

Sara stood and followed me toward the stairs. "Find what you were looking for?" She asked, reaching for the light switch on the wall.

"Don't," I said and shook my head when she shot me a questioning look. Shrugging, she headed down before me. "And yes, I did."

On the first floor, the scene of mom choking me was playing out. I stared at it for a second, feeling the memory of her hands around my throat and the betrayal that had stormed in my heart, even as I knew it wasn't really her. Lowering my eyes, not wanting to remember it, I hurried past and down the stairs, only stopping in the hallway, blinking at the empty house around me. Sara put a hand on my shoulder, and her warmth grounded me. With a weak smile, I led her toward the door, where we dressed and headed out. I locked the door behind me, wanting to keep the house safe when I wasn't there.

"Planning any Samhain decorations this year?" Sara asked as we headed down the steps.

"No," I answered.

"Maybe you should?"

"Why?"

"Well, for one thing, Jack O' Lanterns protects you."

I stopped. "What?"

"Yeah. There's legends around the Lanterns, but we use it as a kind of protection. The light of a Jack O' Lantern'll show the true face of any that step into it, as well as be a beacon for a lost soul."

"I don't really need any more souls in my home, thanks."

We were almost at the gate before she spoke again. "Maybe it'll help find Connor."

When I didn't answer, she wrapped one arm around my shoulders and cuddled her cold nose against the crook of my neck.

At the curb, I pulled from her grip and turned to look up at the house. I'd left the lights on in all the hallways, and they helped. The house looked more alive and inviting now.

Maybe I would carve some Jack O' Lanterns for Halloween, after all. Perhaps I'd even buy some candy and leave the gate open, to see if any of the kids from the neighborhood would dare approach.

3

When we left, the Hearth-house had been filled with the sound of ghosts and sleep. As we entered, the sound of the ghosts was still there, but so was the sound of someone moving around in the kitchen.

The door closed behind us with a click, and the sounds in the kitchen stopped, shortly followed by Mrs. Hearth sticking her head out from the doorway.

"Where have you two been?" she asked before disappearing into the kitchen again.

"At Lizzie's," Sara answered as she pulled off her boots.

Mrs. Hearth appeared in the doorway again and looked at me. "How did it go, dear?"

I shrugged out of my coat. "Fine, I guess."

When I didn't continue, Sara took over. "Lizzie had this idea that maybe a dreamcatcher would help her sleep, and she had one in her bedroom so we went to get it."

Mrs. Hearth nodded. "That might indeed work. Smart thinking. Use your own culture to protect you."

I followed the two Hearth-women into the kitchen, putting the dreamcatcher on the table as I sat, lost in my own thoughts. Mom had been at least quarter Native, and I'd inherited much of that look. I had mom's strong jaw and nose, her high cheekbones, and her full lips. Even my hair was hers, straight and dark brown, almost black. I wore mine in a short bob, though, while she always wore it long. My eyes were my father's, however, blue with spots of green, and big. And my skin was lighter than mom's, almost white enough to look like I just had a tan. It had saved me a lot of trouble in school, and I'd hidden behind it, even as I watched other kids that looked more Native than me be bullied for it. I felt shame move in my stomach.

"It's not, really," I said.

"Not really what, dear?" Mrs. Hearth asked from over by the counter. She was wearing a pale lilac dress with the arms rolled up, and an apron over the front. There were big woolen socks on her feet, and her hair was pulled back from her face in two thin, white braids. She was in her eighties, but her back straight and her arms strong.

"My culture. I don't... I haven't really been part of it, or it part of me, until just this last week or so. I can't call it mine."

Mrs. Hearth stopped working on the dough on the counter and turned to look at me. Sara had pulled a bottle of home-pressed orange juice from the fridge and now stood quietly, holding it and three glasses in her hands.

I pulled the dreamcatcher to me and started fiddling with the feathers. "But I guess I need to do something about it anyway, don't I? I mean, I have all these ghosts hanging around, and I need to help them somehow. According to Jake, it was never a witch's job to deal with ghosts, it was shaman-work, and so none of you really know anything that can help me." Sara opened her mouth but I continued: "Other than to bind them, which is kind of like fixing a broken book with chewing gum. I have to somehow find a way to help me help them, and I'm guessing this is it." I pushed the dreamcatcher away as I said the last words, scowling at it like it was at fault for my current situation.

Mrs. Hearth and Sara moved again. Sara sat in the chair beside me and poured the juice in each glass.

Mrs. Hearth returned to her dough. "How will you do that?"

"Well, the next step would be going to the church where mom was dropped off. That was where we were going yesterday when I remembered... all the ghosts." I looked down at my hands. My fingers were chipping away at my nail polish, and I clenched them into fists.

"While that is all well and good, there is something else that needs to take precedence," Mrs. Hearth said. "Sara, come and help me with these buns, dear."

Sara and I exchanged a glance before Sara stood. "And what's that?" she asked as she went to wash her hands.

"Connor." A chill ran down my spine at Mrs. Hearth's words. "He is now oppressed by a wendigo, a spirit that wants to eat human flesh. We cannot let him run free out there."

Sara joined Mrs. Hearth at the counter and started rolling buns, a furrow in her brow and her lower lip pulled into her mouth to chew on. A heavy silence fell as we all thought our own thoughts. Mine were dark and sad and full of failure.

I looked at their backs. Sara was a little shorter than her grandmother, but her shoulders and hips were just as strong. Where Mrs. Hearth's hair was white and long, Sara's was dyed green and cut short, but they both had blue eyes, and they were both pale white. Sara's face and hands still had faint freckles from summer. Distantly, I wondered if the rest of her was freckled as well, and if it would show through her many tattoos. She used to have freckles all over when she was younger, even places the sun didn't touch.

I walked around and jumped up onto the bench, sitting so I could watch them from the side. "I still want to check out the church today and see if this priest knows anything about mom."

Mrs. Hearth sighed. "If you are leaving for a while anyway, I want to ask Abigail to come by. We should try and talk to her, to explain. Maybe she will calm down."

Sara scoffed, chucking a bun onto the bench with more force than necessary. "Explain? For one, I don't think it'll help. For seconds, I don't think she deserves it. It's not the first time she's pulled this crap, and you know it. Why should she always get the benefit of the doubt when she doesn't give it to the rest of us?"

"Not now, Sara."

"When, then?"

"Not. Now."

Sara snapped her jaw shut and stared at the dough. I opened my mouth to say something but closed it again when I saw the look in Mrs. Hearth's eyes. Stern, but also sad and a little afraid. I remembered what Sara had said the day before. About how Abigail cast her out of the house because Sara wouldn't give up her powers. How Abigail was afraid of her own daughter because of her powers, how she was sure the powers would corrupt Sara, and not giving her daughter the benefit of the doubt.

I stayed where I was, not saying anything as the two women continued rolling the dough.

A clock chimed the half-hour mark from the living room.

"The church is in Dartmouth," I said, trying to talk over the chiming of the clock. "It isn't a long drive, but it is one hour each way, so you would have at least two hours to talk to Abigail."

Mrs. Hearth sighed and closed her eyes for a second. "Well, now that that is settled, why don't you girls help me finish these buns? If we hurry, they should be ready by the time Jake wake up, and we will have a warm breakfast."

4

We spent the next hour creating the vegetarian breakfast of the ages; making homemade buns, scrambled eggs, fruit salad, and even starting a batch of Mrs. Hearth's chocolates. We avoided talking about anything important. No ghosts or monsters, and nothing about mom or Connor or Abigail.

It was a great hour. I only had one problem; I really needed to pee. I hadn't used the bathroom before we left for my place, and I'd been too busy being there to even think about peeing. So why didn't I just go to the bathroom now? Because every time I opened the kitchen door, a flock of ghosts argued for my attention. They didn't say anything, but I could feel their eyes on me, their desperation. Some had been here for generations, stuck, and I was their only hope of getting unstuck.

In the end, I didn't have a choice. I needed to pee, and no way was I doing it in the kitchen sink.

Picking up the dreamcatcher, I drew a deep breath and pushed open the door.

The silence in the hall was absolute and seemed to suck all other sounds out of the house until my own breathing was an echo in my head. Ghosts stood everywhere. Lining the walls and carefully moving out of my path as I rushed past them. They didn't give off any cold, like in the books and movies, but there was a sort of wetness to the air around them. Like mist too fine to see.

My own ghosts were at my side. The twins were walking in front like band sergeants to keep the crowd at bay. Elizabeth and Eleanor were on either side of me, and Magdalena crowding in behind me. I swear I could feel her breath on my hip. The other ghosts followed close behind her, like a veil after a bride. For a moment, I was afraid they'd follow me into the bathroom, but my ghosts stood guard and kept them out after I closed the door.

I almost fell down on the toilet and sighed in relief as my bladder emptied.

When I was done in the bathroom, I made my way to the bedroom I'd shared with first Mark then Sara. The silence of the ghosts hung in the hall, pressing in on me, so I started humming to myself. It wasn't until I was cursing for not being able to hang up the dreamcatcher on my own that I realized I was humming mom's old lullaby. Shivering from the memories, I stopped.

Leaving the dreamcatcher on the nightstand, I went to the bedroom beside mine and knocked on the door. No-one answered from inside.

"Jake?" I called, knocking again. Still no answer. After a third knock, I pushed open the door.

Jake was lying on top of the duvet, fully dressed, and curled into a small ball against the chill of the morning.

I said his name again and walked to his side. He grimaced in his sleep at the disturbance, and for a moment I considered letting him be, but Mrs. Hearth and Sara had asked me to wake him when I went upstairs, so wake him I would.

I shook his shoulder. He grumbled and swatted my hand

away.

"Come on, I know you're awake," I said, not able to keep the smile from my voice.

He opened one grey eye and looked up at me. "No, you don't."

I rolled my own eyes. "Now I do. Come on, we've made buns."

"Buns?"

"Yes. Hurry before they get cold."

I left him as he sat up and stretched, his back and shoulders popping so loud I heard them into the hall.

We were sitting around the table, Sara and I nursing a cup of coffee each while Mrs. Hearth was putting the finishing touches on the table when he joined us. The edge of his too-long brown hair was still wet from where he'd splashed water on his face.

"Why are you all up so early?" he asked around a yawn and slumped into his chair, grabbing the cup of coffee Mrs. Hearth offered him like it was the only thing keeping him alive.

I told him about the morning's adventures as the three others started grabbing for the food. When I was done, they were all well into their first portion. I'd hoped they wouldn't notice I'd not taken anything, but Mrs. Hearth put a still-warm bun on my plate and glared at me until I cut it open and reached for some topping. When I bit into it, I had to fight to keep the food in my mouth, and I realized that the hunger I'd felt while dreaming of the wendigo was gone.

"Well, if you truly have a mental link to it, that is no wonder," Jake said after I mentioned it. "It was hungry, after all, and now it's sated."

"But what about all the other dreams I have? There are other hungry creatures out there."

"Maybe you had a stronger link to the wendigo than the others?"

"But why? And how?"

Jake took a bite of his second bun and chewed, staring into nothing for a moment. "I honestly don't know. I stayed up way past you guys last night, reading and trying to tease out anything I might have missed earlier."

He took another bite of his bun.

"Well? Did you?" Sara asked when he took a third bite.

"No, that's why I'm not saying anything."

She threw a piece of cucumber at him, which he ate with a smile and blew her a kiss.

"So, what do you know?" Sara asked, reaching for another bite of cucumber. Mrs. Hearth grabbed her hand and shot her a stern grandmother-look that made Sara drop the piece with a grin.

"I think the Veil is ruined somehow. That's how all these creatures Lizzie talk about got through to our own plain. I also think Lizzie is the reason the Veil is down, and that's why she dreams of them."

"Ok?" I answered, having managed to force down my second bite of the bun.

"It probably happened when you destroyed the Red Woman. There is an old saying about how the Grey World stands between the Spirit World and us. About it being a last protection from the evils we locked away so long ago. If the Red Woman truly held your ghosts captive there, that pulse of magic you all let loose to destroy her might have been enough to tear a rift in the Veil, letting the spirits on the other side free."

"But you don't know?" Mrs. Hearth asked.

Jake shook his head. "No. There's almost no knowledge about the raising of the Veil or the Grey World. That all happened before witch's sons were allowed to live." The two witches looked down on their plates, shame coloring their cheeks. I couldn't help but see the anger in Sara as her hands knit into fists on top of the table. When she saw me noticing, she hid her hands in her lap. "I also think the Grey World has something to do with necromancers, which is another reason all that knowledge is forgotten," Jake continued.

"Because the witches made sure it was," I said, remembering what he'd told me about necromancers and the witches' fear of them. "Making sure no-one remembers would keep the secret hidden forever."

"Exactly," he said, reaching for his fourth bun, glaring at my own half-eaten one as he did.

"So how do we remember? How do we figure out why I have these dreams, this link as you call it, if even you have forgotten?"

We lapsed into a thick silence as Jake ate another bun, thinking. Sara refilled our coffee cups, and Mrs. Hearth goaded me into finishing the bottom part of the bun. I was feeling a little sick by the time I was done and was happy when Jake spoke up again, hopefully making Mrs. Hearth forget she wanted me to finish the other half as well.

"I think you've already figured it out," Jake said with a smile, pointing at me with the breadknife before he started cutting into his fifth bun. How much could that boy eat?

"Ok?" I asked when he didn't continue.

"Yes. Find a shaman."

"Why?" Sara asked. She was snacking on cucumber now.

"Because the shamans have always kept their cards close to the vest. Witches have purposefully forgotten about the Grey World, how to do anything but support the Veil and anything about spirits except how to bind them. Shamans may not. They may know everything we have forgotten."

I emptied my cup. "Ok, so I need to find a shaman."

"The sooner, the better."

"Guess I should get to it, then," I said, moving to stand, but Mrs. Hearth leaned forward and put her hand on top of mine.

"I am sorry, dear," she began. "But I think that the first thing we need to do is find your father. As we talked about?"

Just the mention of Connor made fear and sorrow stab at my heart, but I swallowed hard and looked at the old woman. Part of me had honestly hoped she'd forget about it. I didn't want to have anything to do with Connor. Especially not now. But if the wendigo coming to our world and taking his body was really my fault like Jake thought? Wasn't it my responsibility to fix it? It was all enough to give me a headache. I could feel it at the back of my mind, growing, and so I tried to stop thinking about it and just focus on the conversation.

"But how? He might be back in Calgary again for all we know!"

"Duh, you're in a house full of witches, Liz, how do you think?" Sara said from the other side of the table.

Mrs. Hearth swatted her granddaughter's arm and motioned to the plates. Sara rolled her eyes.

"And what does that mean?" I asked. I might know they were witches, but I had no idea what they could do other than their active powers, and I didn't even understand half of that. "And shouldn't I try to figure out what to do with the ghosts?"

"Do not worry about that," Eleanor said from the doorway, and I scowled at her. "Right now, your *papa* poses a threat to spirits and humans alike. That must take precedence."

Mrs. Hearth was saying something to the same effect, but the two women's voices melded together to become a white noise that threatened to boost the headache. "...and oppression is nothing to joke about."

"You keep saying ''oppressed''. What does that even mean?"

The two witches exchanged glances, but it was Jake who answered. "Oppressed is when something takes over the body without the original owner's acceptance, like with Connor."

"Usually, we deal with possession, where the owner of the body allows the spirit to use it for some reason or another," Sara continued.

"Oppressions are much more serious," Mrs. Hearth said. "With possession, it can hurt the body but not the soul. Oppression hurts both. The intruder will slowly kill the original soul."

I didn't hear what she said after that. Her last words echoed through my mind again and again. Did that mean Connor was already dead? Or that he was dying? My stomach twisted painfully and I hunched over it. In my chest, the owl was moving, her feathers tickling the inside of my skin, comforting. At my distress, the threads between me and my fright had shuddered in reaction, and they were all in the kitchen now, standing around and looking at me. I could feel their sympathy and worry, and I let those feelings drown out my own fear and sorrow. I couldn't deal with those feelings right now. I couldn't break apart.

"Ok, Connor first," I said in a low voice. "So, you really know a way of finding him?"

"Yes, dear," Mrs. Hearth said as she refilled my coffee mug. By the furrow in her brow, I knew she would have preferred me to drink tea, but we couldn't always get what we wanted, now could we?

"There's a spell," Jake said. "It helps find a lost relative."

"Do witches lose their relatives often?"

"It happens," Sara said.

"Have any of you ever used it before? This... spell?"

Sara and Jake glanced at each other before they shrugged. "All of us, I guess," Sara finished.

Mrs. Hearth seemed to shrink a little. I could see the ghost of a memory flicker across her face. In the memory, tears streaked her face, and her mouth was moving rapidly, saying something too low for me to hear. She looked much younger, in her early forties and not her late eighties.

"So, what do I need to do?" I asked, trying to move the conversation away from the memory hurting Mrs. Hearth.

"You can't do much, dear, but we do need your help." Mrs. Hearth said. "But first, drink your coffee. This may become yet another long day."

I couldn't argue with that.

5

"Usually, I would prefer to do this outside," Mrs. Hearth said as she led us up the stairs. I made sure to walk all the way in the back so that the trail of ghosts following me wouldn't have to walk in the middle of the living. Literally. "But with all the spirits out there, I think we have to do it the old fashioned way."

"Old fashioned way?" I asked Sara as we made our way across the second floor and toward the attic stairs in the back.

Mrs. Hearth stopped in front of the door, almost hidden in the wall, and pulled a key from behind the plant standing on the floor in front of the door.

"Witches had to hide for a long time, so most rituals and such were done indoors. Every witch from grams' generation has a big space for ritual work indoors, hidden from view," Sara answered as Mrs. Hearth opened the door.

I couldn't help but look around in wonder, but there wasn't much to see. The stairs were thin and straight, barely wide enough for one person. The steps and walls were made of uncovered, old wood, but a rug had been laid over the steps to muffle the sound of feet.

Sara ended up walking behind me, and with the stairs as thin as they were, the ghosts had to walk single file as well, and Eleanor made sure to walk just behind Sara, keeping the rest of them from following too close.

"What about our generation?" I asked, following Jake and Mrs. Hearth up the thin stairs.

Sara shrugged as we stopped and waited for Mrs. Hearth to find the second key and unlock the door at the top of the steps. "I usually just do it in the living room. Not like I have to hide from Jake."

At the sound of his name, Jake turned and smiled down at us. "Makes it a lot easier for both of us, and thankfully folks are more accepting of witchcraft these days, thinking it is just New Age stuff."

At the top of the stairs, Mrs. Hearth opened the door and stepped inside, holding it open to let us in.

I hurried up the steps, intrigued despite myself. I'd played a lot in this house, but I'd never been in the attic. After she turned thirteen, Emma used to tease Sara and me that she'd seen the attic, but she never told us where the keys were hidden. When Sara turned thirteen, she said that she also knew where it was, but never showed me. It used to be something we argued about. Not a big argument, but something that came up whenever we were angry at each other. Her not telling me what was in it or showing it to me made me think she didn't trust me.

Turns out, there were many things she didn't trust me with.

The room that opened around me was nothing like I expected. The attic at home was cluttered with old furniture and instruments, albums filled with pictures, paintings, or statues and such made by my family through generations. There were boxes filled with clothing and toys, and suitcases from every era with old diaries or books in them. It was dark, and while not damp, the feeling of dust clung to you long after you'd visited.

The room over Mrs. Hearth's house was anything but that.

The walls were clad in panel and painted white, reflecting much of the light flowing through the three big windows on each wall. Heavy curtains hung on each side, somehow blending in with the white walls. Chests stood along the walls, I guessed filled with witchy stuff, even if I didn't know what that would be. In the middle of the room was a small table covered with a cloth. On the table lay a thick book, two candles, a matchbox, a chalice, a knife, a crystal, and a piece of chalk. A broom lay at the front of it.

I'd heard of altars from New Age friends in Toronto, but nothing like this. The altars my friends talked about had statues and dripping candles and shiny stuff. All the things here looked old and worn.

I was about to tell Sara that it was a little anticlimactic, seeing as there was no obvious witchy stuff here, when a startled yelp made me turn around.

The twins was standing just on the other side of the door, rubbing their noses.

"What happened?" I asked.

Mrs. Hearth, who was about to close the door, stopped and looked at me. "What, dear?"

"We cannot enter," Jonathan answered through his stuffed nose.

When Johana lowered her hand, I saw that her nose was red from where it had hit something.

"The ghosts can't follow," I told Mrs. Hearth.

She blinked at me a moment before realization dawned on her face. "Yes, I imagine they will not be able to enter unless we invite them," she said, turning toward the door. "I am sorry, but this is a protected space. Until we invite you in during a ritual, you can't enter."

"Why did she not say so earlier?" Johana grumbled, rubbing her nose again.

"That is what you get for pushing past everyone," Elizabeth called from further down the stairs.

I couldn't help but snicker.

"Did they get hurt?" Mrs. Hearth asked, looking between me and the, for her, empty doorway.

I cocked my head at the twins, and they shook their heads and turned to walk back down the stairs, but not before I saw the pout on their faces.

"Not really," I said, pushing down a giggle.

The twins scowled at me like it was my fault they'd hurt their noses. Their looks only made my giggle louder.

Behind them, Eleanor sighed and put a hand on each of their shoulders. Jonathan and Johana both stiffened and looked up at her, innocent smiles on their faces.

"Go to your sister," the eldest ghost said, and the twins pushed past her and vanished down the stairs within seconds. Eleanor met my eyes and shook her head with a smile before she started herding the other ghosts down the stairs.

When Mrs. Hearth looked at me, eyebrows raised, I swallowed my giggle and nodded. Mrs. Hearth looked at the now actually empty doorway with a smile on her face that perfectly matched that of Eleanor before she closed and locked the door.

"You guys ready or what?" Sara asked from behind me, and I turned to see she stood by one of the chests. The lid was open, and I saw pouches and mason jars filling it.

As I watched, Sara put four jars down by the altar before she picked up the broom.

"Yes. Dear, sit in front of the altar," Mrs. Hearth said, the last directed at me.

I let her guide me to my spot in front of the altar, my knees touching the area where the broom had lain just before.

"What do I need to do?" I asked, looking up at Mrs. Hearth and pushing my hands between my knees so as not to chew on my nails. What if this didn't work? How would we find Connor then? Not to mention, I was nervous about the mere fact that I was supposed to take part in a witch ritual. Until just a week ago, I hadn't believed any of this even existed, but here I was.

"Right now, nothing," Mrs. Hearth answered and stroked my head, as if to comfort, before she rifled through the book and pulled out a worn piece of paper. "But during the ritual, I need you to do as this note say, ok? I will let you know when. The most important thing, dear, is that you don't say anything else while the ritual is in progress."

I nodded and accepted the note. Even if I wanted to ask more about the ritual, I decided to stop talking from now on until she said it was safe again. I didn't want to risk ruining anything.

Mrs. Hearth stroked my head one more time then moved to sit on the other side of the altar.

Jake had closed the lid of the chest Sara had found the jars in and sat on it, arms crossed and looking on intently.

Sara moved around us, brushing with the broom. I noticed that she walked clockwise and mostly only brushed away a loose circle, not really cleaning. After walking around once, she picked up the chalk from the altar and went to the same spot where she had started and stopped brushing. Staying inside the now clean area, she bent down and drew with the chalk, making sure it kept to the floor as she moved around us until she had drawn a full circle. It was completely round, which was supposed to be impossible. When done with the circle, she started drawing in the air with her finger, mumbling too low for us to hear.

To my shock, I saw the ghost of her golden magic trail the air after her finger, like she was drawing. A five-pointed star took shape, and she drew a circle around it before moving on to draw another one, starting at a different point of the star.

The moment her finger returned to the starting point of the fourth pentagram, connecting the golden lines, it felt like a fresh wind blew over me. I didn't feel my clothes or hair move, but I swear I felt the wind touch my skin and sneak down my shirt. I shuddered, but more from the sudden cold than fear.

Done with the preparations, Sara moved and stood behind me. She didn't mumble anymore. Instead, Mrs. Hearth picked up the matchbox and struck one. The smell of sulfur almost made me sneeze, but I remembered what she'd said and stifled it, my eyes watering from the effort.

As she lit the two candles, she started speaking.

"Spirits, Mother Earth, hear me now.
What is lost, I wish to find.
Help us stop being blind.
Direct me to who I seek.
By Fire, Air, Earth, and Sea.
So mote it be."

The candles lit, she put out the match and lay it on top of the box before she pulled the chalice to her. Lifting the mortar Sara had placed on her side of the altar, she placed it in her lap before plucking herbs from the jars. She placed them all in the mortar and crushed them into the smallest powder she could. When she was done, she placed the mortar on the altar just between us.

"By Fire, Air, Earth, and Sea,
from blood to blood,

we wish to see."

Sara lifted the knife, pulled it from its sheath and handed it to me. The blade was double-edged and dark, made of pure iron. When I didn't do anything, she pointed to the note. I unfolded it for the first time and started reading.

Cut yourself and give three drops to the herbs in the mortar. While you give them, say the following words, then add her name and how she is related to you.

I glared at the note but took the knife. Sara pointed to one of my fingers, and I lay the tip of the blade against it. I really didn't want to cut myself, but the blade was so sharp even just touching it to my skin was enough, and blood welled around the metal. Sara pulled the blade from me and motioned for me to hurry up.

Quickly, I lifted my hand until my finger was just over the mortar, and when the first drop fell onto the herbs, I started the spell.

"By Fire, Air, Earth, and Sea,
from blood to blood,
I wish to see
Connor Joseph Key, my father."

The last of the three drops fell into the mortar, and I pulled my hand back before any more blood could join the soggy mess.

Mrs. Hearth took the mortar as Sara cleaned my finger with a white piece of cloth. The older woman poured water into the chalice before moving the mess from the mortar over to it. She moved it around a little with her fingers until the chalice was filled with a murky grey liquid. As she pulled her fingers out, Sara took the chalice and handed it to me, pointing between her eyes and the content of the vessel.

I took the chalice and looked into the liquid. It still moved in the direction Mrs. Hearth had stirred it, and as it calmed, something else moved within its depths.

Connor. He was dressed just like last night, but blood colored his clothes and face. He was sleeping on the ground, surrounded by polished stonewalls. From somewhere far away came the sound of waves against stones.

I looked up, and before I could stop myself, I said: "I know where he is!"

The spell broke with a snap.

6

"What happened?" I asked and pushed to my feet.

"You broke the spell," Mrs. Hearth said. She sounded resigned, her face seeming drawn and paler than usual.

"How? And are you ok?"

She smiled up at me. "I am fine, dear, just tired." She motioned to the chalice. "Where was your father?"

"In one of the shoreline caves. I don't know which one, but at least we know what area to look in."

"That is good. Jake, Sara, why don't you two go with her, and I will clean up here?"

Jake pushed away from the wall but didn't answer.

Sara had stood almost as soon as the feeling of magic disappeared and was moving around the circle in the opposite direction than earlier. She was removing the glowing pentagrams by tracing them backward. After that, she picked up the broom and brushed the chalk away in the opposite direction. When Mrs. Hearth spoke, she nodded, not pausing her murmuring or movement for a second.

"You're not coming with us?" I asked.

"I need to clean up here. Either way, my powers will not help you with Connor."

"Are you sure? Maybe you could keep him calm or something?"

"Most active powers don't work against spirits," Jake said. He was picking up the jars and putting them back into the chest he'd been sitting on during the ritual.

"He is right, dear," Mrs. Hearth said as she pushed to her feet with a groan. She held the chalice in one hand and bent to pick up the mortar with the other.

"Will you really be ok on your own?" I asked. I felt guilty just thinking about leaving her here.

She flashed me a smile. "Of course, dear. I may be old, but I am not frail." The way she said it, she was challenging me to argue.

"But... I don't want to leave you alone after you spent so much energy on me."

She blinked at me a few times before laughing. "It was not the ritual that tired me out. I have a strong root and can tap into the magic easily enough. That is what a coven leader does. No, your father is what tired me out."

"How?"

"All of this. This last week has been hectic and exhausting for me, just like it has for you. I just need a few hours of mental rest, and getting the three of you out of my house will help with that." She gave me a wink and turned toward the door, but turned back before she'd taken one step. "And bring those ghosts with you. My power may not affect them, but I can sense their emotions everywhere. It is as exhausting as everything else."

"I will." I stammered in surprise.

She nodded and turned, opening the door with two fingers, as her hands were full of mortar and chalice.

As soon as her grandmother was through the door, Sara flung an arm around my shoulders and pulled me tight. I almost fell over, but she kept me up. Looking around, I saw she had Jake in the same stranglehold with her other arm. The young man and I exchanged glances, and I rolled my eyes with a smile.

"I saw that," Sara said and tightened her grip a little. "But no matter! Let's go capture your dad!"

"How?" I asked and pulled away from her. For half a moment, it seemed she wanted to tighten her grip so I couldn't get free, but she finally let me go.

Sara blew a raspberry. "We gotta find him first, right? Why worry 'bout what to do before we have him?"

"Because we don't know anything about how to capture wendigos, that's why," Jake said, pulling out of the stranglehold himself and giving his girlfriend a hard look. "If we go in half-cocked, we might end up getting hurt, or hurting Connor."

"You don't have any idea how to help?" I asked, feeling helplessness move in my stomach.

He shook his head.

I glanced at Sara, who shrugged and moved to sit on one of the chests. I moved with her but glanced out the window instead of sitting down. The sky was still heavy with grey clouds and the street looked deserted. The day seemed to suck the light and life out of everything. Even with the light coming through the windows of my house, it looked eerie. At least the other houses around my own looked the same.

Something white moved across the street, and I squinted, hope fluttering in my chest. Could it be the white crow that had saved me in the Grey World? Mom's soul? Had it come back?

The thing was clearly a bird, and it was white, sitting on the iron gate at the start of the path leading to my front door, but before I could see what it was, the bird fluttered its wings and flew away, disappearing behind the turrets of my house.

I let go a sigh of frustration and relief. What if it really was mom's soul? Did that mean she was captured here like the ghosts? Or could she come and go? Jake had mentioned that there were rituals to reach out to ghosts that had moved on, but I wasn't sure I dared use them. Both mom and aunt Ellie's deaths were too fresh. If I saw them again, I wasn't sure what I'd do. Just the thought of it made my chest hurt. Like my heart was breaking all over again.

Jake cursing drew me out of my thoughts, and I turned back to the attic. He was standing in the middle of the room, just at the edge of the circle Sara had drawn, and was scowling at the altar.

"I don't know," he said and dragged his hands through his brown hair. "As far as my line knows, there has never been a wendigo banishing performed by witches. My best guess is we find Lizzie's grandparents, and they tell us how to banish it."

"But we can't just let it run around out there. What if it hurts someone?" Sara said, gesturing to the window.

"What if it already has?" I said, mostly to myself, remembering a snippet of last night's dream. I suppressed a shudder.

Sara glanced up at me but didn't ask. Instead, she turned back to Jake. "So, what do you want us to do?"

"I think we should try to capture him and bring him back here. That way, at least he won't be able to hurt anyone or himself," Jake answered.

"How? Where could we keep him? In one of the bedrooms?" I asked, not able to keep snark from sneaking into my voice.

Sara snickered, and Jake rolled his eyes. "We keep him up here. There are containment spells Mrs. Hearth can prepare while we're out. When we get him back, he will be subdued by the spells and we can keep him that way until we know how to help him."

"And how do we capture him?"

Sara snapped her fingers. "Mom's crystals. She's some that's used for stunning, not just shields. That way, we stun him and bring him back unconscious."

"She didn't take all her crystals when she left?" I asked.

"Nope, she has a stash in every house she may ever sleep in," Sara stood as she spoke. "Time to go wendigo hunting!" She pushed her hand into the air like she was cheering at some sporting event.

I rolled my eyes and moved toward the door. "Yeah, let's go hunt for my dad. Oh, joy," I mumbled and started down the stairs.

The ghosts had converged at the hidden door, talking over each other to learn what I'd found out. There were so many voices it was near impossible to pick out a single one, so I just stood there, staring at them and letting their voices beat against me. I wasn't sure I could answer even if I wanted to. It felt like the noise drowned my own thoughts. The ghosts didn't quiet down before Sara came down the steps behind me, a reminder of her threat to curse them if they didn't let me figure things out.

Something inside my head snapped back into place, and I was able to speak. As Sara and Jake disappeared down the rest of the stairs, I assured the ghosts I was working on figuring this out as fast as I could. Before they could ask any questions, I followed Sara and Jake down the stairs and hurried into my bedroom. Most of the ghosts seemed to respect that my bedroom and the bathroom were zones where they shouldn't follow me, but they still scowled as I waved my fright in after me and closed the door between them and us.

As I dressed in better clothing – Mrs. Hearth had a stack of thermal underwear and the like lying around, so even if I hadn't brought any with me from Toronto, she'd found some for me and put it out as soon as she was down from the attic – I told my ghosts what we'd found out and what our plan was.

"That is a bad plan," Jonathan said. He and his sister were jumping on the bed, trying to get high enough to get their heads through the ceiling. Their noses weren't red anymore, and I distantly wondered if they could get bumps on their heads. Magdalena had wanted to sit on the bed but gave up as they kept jumping at her and was instead cuddled up close to Elizabeth in the window seat.

I scowled at the twins. "You have a better idea?"

"No," Jonathan answered before he turned and pushed his sister. Johana fell off the bed with a little scream and disappeared through the floor. Elizabeth pushed away from the window with a shout and flew at her younger brother, grabbing him by the ear and forcing him down and through the floor to apologize to his twin sister. I watched them disappear with wide eyes. Even out of view, Elizabeth's shouting rang through the house.

"I guess that just happened," I murmured and looked up at Eleanor and Magdalena. The six-year-old ghost had flown to the last member of my fright when Elizabeth exploded and was huddled close to her. I felt bad for the fear I saw in the girl's eyes. It felt like it was all my fault.

"Do you need us for anything?" Eleanor asked.

"No. I don't want to risk any of you getting hurt by the wendigo again." For a second, the memory of aunt Ellie hung between us. I honestly wasn't sure if I saw the ghost of her fly through the air for real or just before my inner eye, but it stabbed at my chest never the less. I didn't have time to grieve anymore, so I shook my head and walked toward the door. "Mrs. Hearth wanted you all to come with me, so she gets to relax a little, but maybe just stay out of her way? Go back to my place or something? And bring the rest of them as well?"

Eleanor nodded as she stroked Magdalena's hair. The girl was crying again. Probably because of aunt Ellie. I looked away before her tears could spur my own and left the room.

Sara and Jake were already in the hallway, arguing about who should drive. When they didn't as much as acknowledge my presence after I'd put on outer-clothes and was ready to go, I took the keys from Sara's gesturing hand and walked outside, their shocked sounds making me grin despite myself.

Sara and Jake were still arguing as they climbed into the car, but it sounded goodhearted enough. As far as I could gather, they were arguing about who should have worn the purple scarf now around Jake's neck. I rolled my eyes and started the engine.

The drive out to the caves wasn't that long from where we lived. You could easily walk the distance if you had one hour to spare. Sara and I used to sneak out at night and go there, spending the night with only the stars and the ocean as company. Remembering that and knowing things weren't like that anymore made my stomach flip over, but I didn't let myself figure out what it meant. Things had changed. Life always did. One just had to roll with the punches.

Jake and Sara's arguing got thinner and lower in volume until it was all but gone, leaving a heavy silence between us that I was almost afraid to break.

Thankfully, Sara wasn't. "Are your ghosts with us?" she asked, her voice a little weird in the silence, even through the running of the car.

I told her what I'd told the ghosts, and she nodded in reply. Jake spoke up next, walking us through the plan one more time. He was carrying a wooden box, much like the one Abigail had been lugging around yesterday, and as he spoke, he opened it and lifted out a multitude of crystals. They were all rough quartz, and he handed four to both of us girls before putting four in his own pockets.

"Remember, we need to have four of them on the ground and make a cage around him for them to work. If we manage that, he should be stunned, and we can carry him back into the car."

"What if he wakes up while we drive?" Sara asked.

Jake opened and closed his mouth a few times without answering.

I spoke up. "We put him in the trunk and place one stone in each corner. That way, if he wakes up, he should trigger the stones and stun himself, right?"

I glanced at Sara in the passenger seat. I had no idea how these stones worked. She was nodding, though, so I think it was as good a plan as any.

Sara and Jake spent the rest of the drive discussing how best to sneak up on Connor, every now and again, commenting that I should have brought my ghosts so they could scout for us. I only pointed out twice that the wendigo had killed aunt Ellie last night and Sanderson the night before that. No way was I risking that happening to the others before I found a way to help them. None of them argued the point, thankfully.

"It's easy to forget that they can die again, you know?" Sara said, Jake murmuring his agreement and fascination before we returned to the matter at hand.

7

The parking lot was empty except for us: no-one wanted to walk along the ocean when the sky threatened rain. It worked well for us, however.

A cold wind tore through my clothes and settled in my bones. I could feel my owl fluff up her feathers inside my chest, and I buried my nose in the scarf curled around my throat.

"Which way?" Jake asked, stepping up beside me. His hands were in his pockets, but other than that, he didn't look cold at all. I couldn't help scowling a little before I started walking.

After a few steps, Sara hurried up to me and linked her arm with mine.

"You ok?" she asked, snuggling close so we could warm each other. I thought about pulling away, not wanting to seem like I was trying to steal Jake's girlfriend, but looking over my shoulder, I saw he looked as warm and cozy as ever, so I snuggled closer to her instead. When Jake saw me watching, he grinned, and I poked my tongue out at him. Sara saw and did the same before she giggled and bumped me with her hip. "So?"

"About what?" I answered.

"What do you think?"

About the fact that Connor, my dad, was possessed by a

wendigo? That he was back in town? That he wanted to steal my home from me? That I had broken up with Mark? That mom was dead because of me? That I was a shaman and a necromancer, so a woman I had known my whole life wanted to kill me?

Finally, I answered. "I don't know." Sara gave me a look that made me squirm and want to pull away again, but another blast of cold sea-air made me reconsider. "Fine, I'm not fine! How could I be fine? But we can fix this, and then I'll be better, ok?"

She didn't answer but cuddled even closer. At this rate, we would end up tripping each other.

Just as I thought it, the thin path we'd been following opened up. The scraggly trees and brush that had so far hidden the view disappeared, letting us see the ocean. It was just as grey as the sky above, and the waves were topped with white foam as they rolled against the stony beach before us. Small cliffs rose up on both sides. Southward, they would fall away until they lay flat again and gave us the woods and hill that created Sky Harbour. Toward North, the cliff rose up until it was a small, steep mountain. That was the way we were going.

When the cliffs were created, they must have been underwater, for the caves were long and thin, the walls polished smooth from the currents that had made them. So even if I hadn't heard the ocean against the rocky beach when I looked into the chalice, I would have recognized the sleek walls of those caves. The only problem was knowing which one Connor was in. There were seven of them, a few of them connected by thin cracks that hardly even a child could squeeze through, and three of them lay mostly or partly underwater when the high tide was in. It was currently low tide, and that meant Connor could be in any of the caves for hours yet.

As if reading my mind, Sara asked. "Where do we start?"

"On the top and work our way to the bottom?" I asked.

Jake shook his head. "He may hear us and know we're coming. We should move from the bottom up, always leaving one of us outside as a guard in case he tries to run away."

"Guess you wanna be the guard?" Sara asked, her voice so soft I thought she might not want me to hear.

I glanced from her to Jake, who met my eyes.

"I don't like tight spaces," he said, wrapping his arms around himself.

"Then you're the guard," I said. "I can't really climb right now, but there should be paths up to each cave. I haven't been here in years."

"Me neither," Sara answered, and for a second, she flickered before my eyes. This time to summer clothes, her dyed dark hair pulled back in a ponytail revealing her pale shoulders. She was grinning at me and tugging at my hand to hurry me along. Then she flickered back to her current self. Her short, green hair was whipping back and forth in the ocean wind, and her hand was moving from my arm to my hand, wrapping her fingers with mine. She was smiling that grin she used when we were doing something we knew we weren't supposed to. Her joy was infectious, and I could feel her warmth through our gloves, slipping up my arm to nestle in my chest.

"Time to hunt us a wendigo, then!" The grin never left her face.

As we stepped off the hard earth and onto the stones, Sara let her magic run free.

Apparently, there were no spells that would muffle the sound of moving people, but Sara's luck should go a long way to keep us from making too much noise. At least in theory.

"You should really create a quiet spell," I groaned to Jake

when I almost fell over as a stone rolled away from under me. Trying to walk this quiet was torture for my nerves; they were already on high alert these days.

"I'm thinking," he answered, helping me to my feet again.

"Is he serious?" I asked Sara.

She shrugged. "Probably. His interests aren't in making new spells like his mentor, but he has a lot of knowledge on the subject."

"Why hasn't anyone made a quiet spell before?"

"Because there's a lot of factors to consider," Jake said from just at the edge of the golden bubble that was Sara's magic. I wasn't sure if they could see it, but Jake managed to stay within. Maybe that was the luck at work? "There are spells to hide sound when you stand still, even make you invisible, but none that work perfectly when you move. Sound is even harder than hiding yourself, as you have to consider the environment around you as well. 'tis simple science."

I glanced at Sara. "I thought you said magic wasn't science?"

"Well," she dragged the word. "It is and it isn't?"

"That doesn't make sense."

"What Sara means is that magic is bound by laws that reflect what we call science today. And many of the things we know today were called magic in the past. Who's to say what we call magic today won't be science in a few years?" Jake answered.

"You guys are giving me a headache with all this stuff," I mumbled.

"It makes sense, if you think about it," Jake continued.

I didn't answer as I focused on not stepping between two big stones and risk getting my leg trapped. The walking was pure pain on my sore and battered body, and I was considering asking if they knew any healing spells – what use were witches if they couldn't do at least that much? – but decided against it and just focused on moving my legs in a way that would keep me upright. When I almost fell again, Jake reached out a hand. When I looked up, he smiled and nodded, so I grabbed hold of his lower arm and let him support me across the stones. He smelled like charcoal and erasers, mixed with the scent of old books and Mrs. Hearth's chocolates. Beneath that was his own cinnamon smell.

Finally, we made it to the foot of the cliff and huddled down behind a scraggly bush.

After a short conference, Sara snuck out from behind the bush first and moved until she was at the edge of the first cave. I followed, leaving Jake to stay partly hidden in case Connor tried to sneak away while we were inside the caves.

When I reached her, I saw that Sara had one crystal in each hand, so I followed her lead. I really wanted to take her hand and clutch to it as a lifeline, but we didn't have time for that.

Exchanging a look, we both nodded, and Sara sprang to the other side of the opening on quiet feet. Her aura of luck still reached me, but just barely, so I stepped out to make sure it touched me.

Staying on each side of the opening, we headed into the cave.

The scent of stale saltwater and wet stone assaulted my nose, and I had to concentrate not to sneeze. Sara was letting loose some muffled groans, so I guess I wasn't the only one.

If the sun had been out, we would have been able to move through the cave without a problem, but it wasn't, which left the inside of the cave in darkness, looking like a hole where there shouldn't be one.

Putting away one of my crystals, I pulled out my phone and turned on the flashlight app. I heard Sara say something, but not exactly what. Instead of turning to her, I shone the light deeper into the cave.

A few more steps and the floor started falling down.

Me in front, our steps throwing wet echoes against the walls around us, we walked to the lip and looked down. Green water lay like a mirror in front of us, stretching across the floor to the back of the cave, where the wall disappeared into the murky depths.

"Guess this is the wrong cave," I mumbled and turned to Sara.

She cursed as I shone the light in her eyes and turned around, almost slipping on the slimy floor. I reached out, but she was too far away for me to support her. Her luck was still going strong, however, so she somehow managed to keep on her feet.

"Sorry," I mumbled and shone the light on the ground as she turned to glare at me.

"Better be," she said, but I saw the shadow of her tongue as she stuck it out at me. "Let's go."

I nodded and turned off the app, wanting to save the battery.

Despite not walking deep into the cave, the fresh air of the outside was like a whole other world compared to the dampness within. Almost like the misty cold of the ghosts, I realized as Sara led the way to the next cave after waving to Jake.

We followed a small strip of hard earth and crushed shells along the cliff, the sea drawing ever closer until we reached the second cave. It lay a little higher than the first one, but only by a few centimeters.

Its entrance was smaller than the first, and we had to stoop to walk through while the inside opened up so we could stand straight. The smell of stale water was here as well, but also something else. Something musky, like wet dog.

I turned on my light and moved into the cave, clutching the

phone so hard the plastic creaked in protest.

This cave was deep and tilted down, but while the walls, floor, and ceiling were covered in algae, there was little water. The slide to the bottom was short, maybe just two meters, but better safe than sorry, so we sat down and pushed down the small hill. I grimaced at the feel of algae under my fingers and the wet feeling of my jeans-bottom. Sara was mumbling something under her breath that sounded strangely like a curse. I wondered if witches could actually curse someone by cussing.

I stood as soon as my feet hit the ground and looked around, my light bouncing against the walls. Because of the bouncing, I almost missed it, but Sara's gasp made me freeze.

"What?" I whispered, not daring to move.

Instead of answering, she walked over and took the hand with the phone, carefully moving it until the cone of light hit what I'd overlooked.

There was a puddle of stale water in one corner, but instead of being a green color as the water in the first cave had been, this one was brown, almost red if the light hit just right. What I had missed but Sara had seen was a hoody against the back wall. There was no way for us to getting there without wading through the water, and we had no idea how deep it was, but the hoody seemed to be half-submerged and stuck on something. It was mostly a rusty brown color, but here and there was a bright blue streak or patch.

"You think..." I began but wasn't able to finish.

When I glanced at Sara, she was shaking her head. Not knowing the answer or not wanting to know? I didn't ask. I wanted to argue that the hoodie could have been down here for a while, but it didn't show signs of the water having worked on it long. The rust-like color could just be paint, or the blue could be paint. But even as I thought it, there was a little voice in the back of my head that murmured that I had eaten someone in my dream last night. That I'd cracked his head open with a rock. Had he been wearing a hoodie? I couldn't remember. Gorge rose in my throat and I had to swallow hard to keep it down.

"Let's get outa here," Sara said. Her low, shaking voice broke through my thoughts. "He's not here, but he could've moved to one of the higher caves after..." she couldn't finish, couldn't even look at the hoodie. I didn't dare speak, afraid I would throw up, but she continued. "We'll call the police when we're on our way home. Say we found it when showing Jake the caves. They can look into it."

I nodded. My hand was gripping the crystal so hard it hurt, so I put it in my pocket. Sara's hand found mine and I squeezed it, feeling it shake slightly. My own hands were completely steady, but they felt huge and unruly, like they weren't really mine.

Together, we turned to climb the incline.

My light fell on the crooked wall in front of us and the breath caught in my throat. Sara froze half a second after me, her hand gripping mine so hard it hurt.

Our asses had made big holes in the algae as we slid down, but there were other marks as well. Footprints and what looked like drag marks. Like someone or something had slid down it, bringing something huge – like a body – with it, and then climbed out alone.

8

By the time we were out of the cave, we were both shaking. I had managed not to throw up, even if the dry-heaving had hurt my ribs so much I had trouble breathing properly even now. Sara had kept it together better, but she kept sniffling and turning her face away.

With Sara's help, I was able to hobble my way along the small path back to where we'd left Jake. When he noticed, he came out of hiding and ran to us, almost slipping on the wet stones.

"What happened?" he whispered as he reached us, hand going toward Sara's face. When she shook her head, he changed course and took my other arm instead, supporting it as best he could. "Did you find him?"

"No," Sara said, and when Jake opened his mouth to ask, she shook her head. He closed his mouth and helped her help me to the spot where he'd been sitting.

When I sat on the ground, back against the chill cliff but somewhat hidden from the wind, Sara told Jake what we'd found. His face went from interested to shocked to deathly pale.

"That is not good," he said when she was done.

"No shit," I murmured, still breathing heavily but calmer now that we'd stopped moving, and I wasn't shivering from both fear and cold. Just fear now, thanks, and maybe some sorrow.

"We need to call the police," Jake said, reaching for his phone, but Sara took his hand and pressed it to her chest instead.

"I know," she said when he shot her a worried look. "But we can't let them know we've found nothing before we find Connor. If the police find him, who knows what'll happen." Jake lowered his gaze. "When we've got Connor, we call the police and tell them we were showing you the caves and found the hoodie."

"In this weather?" Jake waved to the choppy, grey waves and the heavy sky.

"Many people come out here for windy weather like this, wanting to see the waves and ocean in the wild winds," I said, my voice monotonous and empty. "I think the only reason no-one else is here now is because of the heavy clouds. We're lucky."

Sara nodded. "We'll look in the upper caves. You stay here and rest. If Connor comes, scream."

I gave a shaky laugh and nodded.

Sara forced a smile and gave me a wink before she dragged Jake out from behind the bush and went back the way we'd come.

The path went up along the cliff in a zig-zag form, arriving at every cave. People had wondered about the path for generations, but no-one had ever owned up to making it. There had been talk of closing it off, but they soon realized the only way to do so would be to blow up the front of the cliff, and no-one wanted that. Instead, they installed a handrail after the second cave so people would at least have something to hold on to if they wanted to brave the slippery path, and there was a warning sign back at the parking lot, so the town and state couldn't be held responsible if something happened.

It felt like I sat behind that bush for an eternity. Even if I was mostly hidden from the wind, it seemed to find its way around the bush and into my clothes. It nestled there before it started burrowing into my skin and flesh, and it soon felt like it was in my bones.

Getting to my feet, I walked to the water's edge and turned.

The cliff rose up, the upper caves hidden because of the angle from where I was standing. I could see the railing, dark wood against the grey stone, but couldn't see Jake or Sara.

"Please be ok," I prayed to a god I didn't believe in as I tried to guess which cave they were in. I wasn't sure if I was praying for Sara and Jake, or for Connor. What would happen when they found him? If he was even here, would they be able to subdue him? What if he hurt one of them?

As if the world had read my thoughts, a yell sounded from the cliffs. It was so far away that the wind almost hid it from me, but because I was listening for a sound, any sound, I got it. My eyes jumped to the fifth cave, at least fifty meters over the ground. It looked small from my perspective, and the view sent a chill running over my arms and down my back. What was going on in there?

When nothing else happened right away, I started walking toward the path. I'd barely taken three steps, eyes still on the cave, when something moved in the opening. I saw Sara's bright green hair against the dark before she went flying out of the opening, back first. For half a heartbeat, she hung in the air before she started falling.

I called her name and rushed forward, my own helpless outburst echoed by Jake's yell and Sara's own scream of terror.

Before I'd taken three steps, Sara was swallowed by the waves, her golden magic disappearing with her.

Water splashed over my legs as I ran into the ocean, adrenalin making me overlook the freezing temperatures and forget the pain of my ribs.

"Lizzie!"

Jake's yell forced me to turn in time to see someone push past him and rush down the path.

I followed Connor with my eyes. He was dressed as he had been last night, but his white shirt looked almost black with blood, and blood stained his hands and face.

A splash made me turn around, and I saw Sara swim toward shore. Forgetting Connor for a second, I wadded toward her, the waves trying to push me back.

By the time we reached each other, our teeth were chattering in tandem. Sara's hands were cold when I gripped them, and the cold instantly transferred to my skin, reminding me of the wet atmosphere hanging around ghosts.

With my help, Sara pushed to her feet and immediately started pulling me toward land, her eyes glued to Connor as he rounded the last bend on the path. He was much faster than I could believe my father to be, and he was running in a way that made it look like he wasn't quite sure how best to move his own body—back hunched and arms flapping forward like he really wanted to be on all fours. His legs were pumping hard, knees stiff and muscles tense against the fabric of his jeans. It looked like he was hurting himself.

"The crystals," Sara gasped between chattering teeth before she let me go.

My hands shot into my pockets, finding the quartz hidden there, a little warm despite the wet fabric of my clothes.

Gripping them, I made my way onto the shore just as Connor reached the bottom of the path. He rushed at me, faster now that he was sure not to slip and fall. I wanted to yell for him to stop, to ask him to fight it, but as our eyes met, I knew that wouldn't help. His eyes were all black. There was nothing of Connor left. Something tugged at my heart, and I felt a lump form in my throat.

"Now!" Sara and Jake called in unison.

I threw the two crystals toward the wendigo. At the same time, Sara threw one from where she was standing in the water, and Jake dropped one from above, leaning as far over the edge of the path as his grip on the railing would allow.

Connor lowered his head and pushed more speed into his legs, and for a second, I was sure we would miss him. He lifted his arms, a grin showing too many teeth split his face in half as his fingers curled to form claws ready to rip and tear at me.

Jake's crystal hit the ground and the moment it made contact with the earth, it flashed. The other crystals surrounding Connor in an uneven box flashed, and lightning ran between them and arced up, reaching for Connor like chains thrown at an animal.

I stumbled back as one of his hands passed over the invisible line between the two crystals I'd thrown, a glint of triumph in his eyes.

The lightning grabbed at him. It moved up his body and form a collar around his throat. It ran inside his muscles and force him to stand still and spasm in place. For a moment, I saw a shadow around his body. It was the shadow of a hulking beast not of this world, and it reached its hands toward me, four fingers with too many joints splayed as it begged for... what? Mercy? Or was it just raging against the limitations of the body it had chosen?

Connor fell to his knees, still trembling from the lightning moving through him, but his eyes rolled back and the grin was gone from his face. He fell forward, hitting the stones with a crunch that made me wince. The lightning fizzled into nothing as soon as he lay still.

Sara walked out of the water and to my side. She lay her arms around me and drew me close, sharing my body heat while her own body shook from cold and adrenaline.

"How did you survive that fall?" I asked, wrapping my numb arms around her and not taking my eyes off Connor's quiet form. "The beach is too shallow for anyone to survive that fall."

"I'm just lucky that way," she managed between chattering teeth, and when I glanced at her, she was grinning madly.

9

Staying out in the cold would land Sara and me sick long before the police arrived, so Jake and Sara carried Connor to the car while I picked up the crystals we'd used to capture him. When I reached the car, Connor was in the trunk with crystals in each corner. If he woke, he would knock himself out the moment he moved.

Jake took the wheel and drove home while Sara called Mrs. Hearth to inform her we were on our way. She undressed while she talked until she was left sitting in her underwear in the front seat, the heaters on full blast, leaving her wet clothes in a soggy mess on the floor. Her tattoos looked unreal against her almost blue skin. I followed her example and pulled off my wet pants and socks.

As we drove, we agreed not to call the police at all. There should be no proof of our visit to the caves, at least not after the high tide came in. There might still be blood and such from Connor in the higher caves, but there wasn't anything we could do about that. If Connor had killed the owner of the hoodie, the victim's family deserved justice, but how could they get it against a spirit-creature like a wendigo? When I asked Jake, he didn't know. He feared the only way for the family to get any form of resolution was for Connor to take the blame.

I thought about arguing. Argue that Connor hadn't really done anything, but I couldn't bring myself to do it. To the rest of the world, Connor had killed someone.

The memory of his grin as he came toward me flashed every time I closed my eyes. The sight of something stuck between his teeth that looked like uncooked chicken skin made my stomach churn and bile rise in my throat.

Shuddering, I forced my eyes open and looked out the window, trying not to blink and swallowing heavily.

As Jake stopped the car, Mrs. Hearth stepped out on the porch, a tray in her hands.

Before I was even out of the car, my fright of ghosts was there as well, standing just far enough away that none of us mortals would risk walk right through them. The twins were talking excitedly and asking questions while their older sister tried calming them down, but I didn't have the energy to deal with any of them right now. They must have noticed, feeling my empty sorrow through the threads between us, for they stayed back, giving me the space I needed.

Mrs. Hearth rushed to the car and pushed cups of something steaming into all our hands before she removed the blankets she had over her shoulders and wrapped them around Sara and me.

"You two get inside," she said as she picked up a small leather bag from the tray. "Jake and I will get Connor."

Sara took my hand and dragged me toward the house. Her lips were blue and she was shivering, but at least her hand felt warm against my skin. It probably wasn't a good thing that I couldn't feel the chill of the ground under my naked feet, so I was glad when Sara pulled me toward the burning fire in the living room and plumped us both down on the carpet in front of it.

Mrs. Hearth had put a trey with a kettle that was still steaming and smelled much like the concoction in our cups – it was spicy and warm and bitter, but it worked – as well as warm clothes on a side-table.

As soon as we were dressed, Sara pulled me under the blanket together with her. I considered finding my own blanket, but I also knew the best way to heat up was body heat, so I let her wrap her arms around me and rest her head on my shoulder, skin against skin.

Glancing over my shoulder, I saw that we were completely alone. I turned my head and smelled Sara's hair. It was salt from the ocean and smelled like the autumn wind, but beneath that was her own smell. Like warm milk and honey. The way she had always smelled.

The scent filled my chest with warmth, and at the same time it made my back stiffen. She wasn't mine anymore, just like I wasn't hers. We shouldn't be sitting like this. But I couldn't pull out from under the blanket either. Instead, my hand found hers. She took it and braided her fingers in-between mine, holding tight. I didn't pull away, but leaned my head on hers instead, feeling her hair tickle my cheek. Warmth blossomed in my lower stomach and spread.

The door opened and I lifted my head to watch Jake come in, Connor flung over his shoulder in a fireman's carry. Jake didn't even glance our way but focused on moving forward. His lips were pulled into his mouth in concentration, and his face was red from the weight.

The twins and Elizabeth followed after him, the twins staring at Connor with a mix of fear and excitement, their sister trying to hold them back but not succeeding. The other ghosts entered the living room and stood back, as if respecting the fact that we needed to warm up and their energy wouldn't help.

Mrs. Hearth was the last inside. "Warmed up?" She asked as she stepped out of her shoes.

We nodded, and she gave a small smile before she hurried up the steps after the two men.

"What if they were seen?" I asked.

"They were not," Eleanor said at the same time as Sara answered: "Grams used a mirror spell, so no-one saw nothing."

"A mirror spell?" I asked, glancing at the ghosts.

"She puts up a mirror image of the house, so everyone looking would see the house as it was when she prepared the spell," Sara said, taking the last sip of her tea and reaching for the clothes. She pushed some into my hands as well. Still under the blankets, we dressed.

Finally, we sat fully dressed in front of the fire, our shoulders touching.

"Should we go up and help them?" I asked.

Sara shook her head. "You can't do nothing."

I wanted to argue but knew she was right. I wasn't a witch. I hadn't even been a shaman for more than a week. What did I know?

After a long while, Jake came down the steps, the three ghosts following him. He sank down on the floor beside Sara and rested his head on her shoulder. She kissed it at a weird angle and stared into the flames again.

The twins were nagging me to tell them what had happened, but I didn't know how to articulate what happened at the caves. It should have been easy to explain that we found him and captured him, but I couldn't. Instead, I remembered the hoodie, and my jaw sealed shut.

Noticing my discomfort, Elizabeth grabbed the twins by the ears and marched them out of the living room. Eleanor followed, resignation on her face. When Magdalena realized she would be left alone with us, she glanced between me and the wall the other ghosts had disappeared through. I gave her a small nod, and she flew after the rest of the fright. I could hear the twins muffled voices protesting and saying they were in pain for a long time, until Eleanor's voice rose once, sharp as a whip. The quiet that followed was only broken by the three of us breathing and the crackling of the fire.

We sat there, each in our own thoughts, until Mrs. Hearth joined us. With her, she brought a tray filled with leftovers from breakfast, and more tea to heat us up.

"How is he?" I asked as I accepted the plate she all but pushed into my lap.

"He is fine for now, dear," Mrs. Hearth answered, not meeting my eyes.

"What'd you do to him?" Sara asked, lifting her head from my shoulder and yawning.

"Tied him up in a circle in the attic. He will be asleep until I undo the spell," Mrs. Hearth answered, throwing another log on the fire.

"So, he's safe?" I asked.

"He is safe."

"Good." I wasn't sure if I meant it or not. I was still angry at Connor for leaving me, then showing up the way he had, but that didn't mean I wanted him to suffer either. It was all one big mess of emotions I had no idea what to do with.

We ate in silence for a while. Jake and Sara ate a lot, arguing over the best piece, and Mrs. Hearth managed to threaten me into eating half the bun on my plate. By the time we were done,

I was warm and sated.

"Abigail called while you were out," Mrs. Hearth said when Sara and Jake started slowing down. "She wanted to come over for dinner."

"U–hu," Sara answered, her earlier happy face falling into emptiness. "I'm sure she does. She coming alone or bringing the whole coven?"

"She said she was coming alone," Sara narrowed her eyes at her grandmother. "But either way, I would suggest that Lizzie and Jake drive to Dartmouth and have a look at that church."

Sara nodded her agreement, her tense shoulders relaxing a little.

"Why? You don't think she'd try to kidnap us or anything, do you?" I asked, trying to lighten the mood, but the three serious faces turning my way made me reconsider my words. "She would?"

"I told you she's gone mad," Sara said, lying down on the rug and stretching until her back popped.

"So, she'd try to kidnap us while supposedly eating dinner with her mom and daughter?"

"U–hu."

I opened and closed my mouth a couple of times before nodding. Great. Now I had to be afraid of witches kidnapping me as well. That was just fantastic. When Sara told me Abigail wanted to burn me, that she tried to talk the rest of their coven into it, I didn't really believe her. At least, part of me hadn't believed it. Now, that part shut up and went to sit in a corner.

"But why burn me? Isn't that what folks used to do to witches?" I asked.

"Yes," Jake answered. "But the Christians had it right. Fire is one of the best cleansers in the world."

"Cleanser?"

"Something that removes magic," Mrs. Hearth answered. "The elements are better than most everything else. Running water or living flame is best."

I opened and closed my mouth a couple of times before I was able to say something. "So Abigail thinks she can... cleans me?"

"'tis not for you," Jake said, not looking at me. "She wants to cleanse your energy, your soul, from this world so it won't affect the magic here."

"Oh," I said.

For a moment, no-one said anything. I felt completely numb, like I wasn't really here. But something was moving in my chest. The owl? Sorrow? Fear? I wasn't sure anymore. I had felt too much these last two weeks, and I wasn't sure I could feel any more.

Without a word, I pushed to my feet.

"Lizzie?" Sara's voice seemed far away.

I wasn't able to answer. Instead, I left the living room and its inhabitants behind and hurried up the stairs.

10

I stayed in that empty void as I walked up the stairs, hardly seeing or hearing my ghosts as they tried to talk to me. They were just noise and cold against my skin, and I wasn't sure I could take it.

Taking the last two steps at once, I hurried into the bathroom and slammed the door behind me, hoping they would respect it. They did.

I put my back against the door for a moment, drawing a deep breath, finally feeling something. It was relief, but even that feeling was muted.

From below, I could hear Sara's voice. She raised it once before the house fell into silence. Even the ghosts outside the door had stopped speaking. I could feel them standing there, like a wall of mist, and I could feel the worry thrumming through them. Worry and some fear, but I wasn't sure what they were afraid of. Me? Or the spirit in the attic?

I bit back a hysterical laughter and stumbled to the counter. My hand was moving toward the faucet, but I didn't feel it. It was like I watched someone else control my body. The sound of running water drowned out the ghosts feelings, and I splashed it onto my face, skin puckering with the cold and finally making me feel again. My hands were cold, my face was cold, and the water dripping down my shirt was cold. And it touched my skin, which was mine and mine alone. And I wasn't evil, no matter what Abigail thought.

Someone knocked at the door, and I heard Sara's voice through the wood, asking how I was doing. Without answering, I unlocked the door and stepped back. Sara slipped inside and closed it behind her.

Sara hardly looked at me before she turned off the water, found a towel, and pulled me to the floor. Sitting between my legs, she patted my face dry with the towel.

Suddenly, I desperately wanted to cry. I wanted to cry myself to sleep and forget this whole day. Forget the last week or even the last five years. I wanted everything to be back to the way it was before mom got sick or even before Sara had that fight in high school, and we broke up. Things were so much simpler then.

"Hey," Sara said. She'd stopped patting my face, but it was still wet. I hadn't been able to keep the tears at bay after all. That only made me cry harder. "Hey," Sara said again, putting away the towel and hugged me. She carefully kissed away my tears and shushed me until my sobs quieted down. "This sucks, doesn't it?" she asked when my tears finally stopped falling.

I couldn't help the hiccuppy laugh that escaped me. Sara laughed with me before letting me go.

Still holding my hand, she sat down beside me and leaned her shoulder against mine. I dried the last of my tears and leaned my head against her shoulder.

"It really sucks," I whispered to her.

She was caressing my hand with her fingers, and I closed my eyes, focusing on that feeling.

"We could run away," she said. "Just slip out at midnight and escape deep into the woods. We can live in a cottage and survive on what we can grow and hunt ourselves. It could be just like it used to be. Just the two of us."

I wanted that so much it hurt. "What about Jake?"

"He can come too."

"Wouldn't he be jealous?"

"'bout what?"

"About the two of us being just like we used to be?"

She chuckled. "He wouldn't mind as long as he could join every now and again." My fingers twitched in hers, and her chuckle died. "He knows almost everything 'bout us, you know. 'bout what we used to be to each other. What you still are to me."

I lifted my head and turned to look at her. "And that is?"

She cocked her head, a sad smile on her lips. "You know that."

I shook my head, about to say that I didn't. She was the one who broke us up. It hurt so bad when it happened, even if I was thankful. We hadn't been ourselves since that night, but I never quite knew why she ended it. Now I knew it was because of her magic. Because she was a witch and she didn't want me to know it was because of her power that she won that fight and almost killed a boy. Even if he tried to rape me. I opened my mouth to ask anyway, but before I could, she leaned close and touched her lips to mine.

I froze for a moment, shocked, before I closed my eyes and kissed her back. Her fingers squeezed my hand and lifted it up between us, pressing it between her breasts. Her other hand found my cheek and rested there. I wrapped my free arm around her waist, pulling her as close as I could. Her tongue touched my bottom lip, and I wanted to suck her in, to be as close as one could be to another person.

Instead, I pulled away and rested my forehead against her shoulder so I didn't have to look at her. Her hand slipped from my cheek and over my head, resting at the nape of my neck.

"I'm sorry," I said, panting. "I shouldn't have done that. You're in a relationship and..."

My words died away. I wasn't sure what I was going to say next. She was the one who kissed me, so why was I apologizing?

She kissed my temple. "I'm sorry. It's my fault. I just... I've missed you for so long, and now you know everything, and you're so sad, and I want to be there for you."

"What about Jake?"

She chuckled. "Didn't I just tell you he knows everything 'bout us?"

I lifted my head and looked her square in the eyes. "But you're in a relationship with him. You live together."

She leaned forward and touched her nose to mine. "There are many kinds of love. Jake and I... we're best friends and great in bed," I blushed, and Sara giggled, moving her nose to the other side of mine, breathing slowly against my cheek. I had to suppress a shiver. "But we're not exclusive. He knows I'm more interested in women than in men. He knows I dream of another woman every now and again. We've talked 'bout what we'd do if I ever fell for another woman." She moved her nose along my cheekbone, brushing her lips against my jaw.

I leaned my head back, wanting to drown in her, but just as I was about to let everything go, the door banged against our shoulders.

Sara jumped with a squeal, and I slammed my head against the counter. Sara's squeal turned to a muffled laugh.

"You ok in there?" Jake asked, and my grimace of pain fell before I giggled. Sara giggled right along with me. "Hello?

Sara? Lizzie?"

"Yes," I finally answered. "We're fine, thanks."

"You sure? You sound funny."

"It's nothing," I managed before burying my mouth against Sara's shoulder, trying to drown the laughter before he could hear it. It wasn't really that funny, but all the feelings moving through my body needed a release, and laughing was better than crying.

"Ok," Jake answered after a second, not sounding convinced.

"We're fine, Jake. Go back downstairs," Sara said, her voice somewhat steadier than mine.

"If you're sure," he said. "I'm here if you need anything."

My laughter died, and I stared at the door for a heartbeat. "Thank you," I finally said, meaning it with all my heart.

Beside me, Sara had stopped laughing as well and was looking at me. "What do you need?"

I couldn't look at her as I pushed to my feet. "Just a few moments alone, if that's ok?"

She scrambled up. "Of course. You shouldn't have to ask."

Forcing a smile, I stepped to the door and opened it. Jake stood outside, a furrow in his brow, but before he could say anything, Sara slipped past me and took his hand.

"Come on," she said in a hushed voice. "Let's give her some room."

"You're telling me," he murmured as she pulled him down the stairs.

What now? I considered going back into the bathroom, but my eyes fell on my hands. I was chipping away at my nail polish again, and that gave me an idea. The one thing that always calmed me down.

11

The small black bag was hidden at the bottom of my suitcase.

With earbuds in my ears blasting music from my iPod, I opened the bag and arranged its content across the desk. Nail cleaning and care supplies, thin brushes, tweezers, paper napkins, and the like went to the far left. Then the many bottles of nail polish right in front of me, with the clear cover gel standing to the right, together but apart, and the UV drier all the way to the right.

Drowning in the music, I cleaned and tried to shape what was left of my nails after I'd bitten them all to the quick. I had to open the window so I wouldn't choke on the smell of acetone. Before I started painting them, I plugged in the UV drier and took a moment just to breathe.

Just this little action had calmed me already. The moment I stopped, though, the by now well-known exhaustion, fear, and sorrow returned, and I hurried to push it down by grabbing a random bottle of nail polish.

I used near an hour fixing up my nails, forgetting everything else for a moment, just concentrating on the music and the movements. In the end, I'd put on a metallic black that shone in the weak light coming through the window. The black felt too morose, even with my mom's funeral just two days before, so I used one of the smaller brushes to paint gold vines across the nails on my left hand. The vines spread over the pinky, ring finger, and middle fingernails, ending in a metallic red bloom on the next finger over, leaving only the thumb pure black. I considered doing the same on the other hand as well, but I'd always liked the idea of doing art on just one hand, so I left it.

After it dried, I photographed it with my phone and added it to my Instagram account.

After putting all the nail supplies away, I leaned back in my chair and hummed along to Dua Lipa's song *New Rule.* When the song was over, I turned off the music and pulled out the earbuds. The time spent thinking about something else had cleared the fog of emotions that filled my mind, and I felt ready to face the next step of the day: Going to Dartmouth and finding the church where mom was left as a baby.

Even just thinking about it made the feelings stir again, but I was calm enough to control them now.

I slipped out of the bedroom, feeling more like me than I had in a while, and headed down the stairs, taking care to not step on the boards that creaked. The ghosts were gone from the hall, but I could feel my fright in the sunroom, so I slipped past it as quietly as I could, not wanting them to know I'd emerged from the bedroom.

As I neared the kitchen, voices drifted through the open door.

"Because we should try and help those that don't know any better," Mrs. Hearth said.

"She should know better! You raised her more than you raised Emma or me, and we've turned out better than her," Sara answered with a sharp voice.

"Really, dear?"

"That's not fair, and you know it."

I leaned toward the door, trying not to be seen and looking in and at the same time,.

Jake and Mrs. Hearth sat at the table, and Sara sat on the counter, tearing a piece of paper into tiny bits.

Mrs. Hearth stood and walked to the counter. She took a bowl of chocolates from a cupboard and sat it on the table and motioned for Sara to join her.

Sara scowled, but jumped down from the counter and sat at the table.

No-one said anything as they did, until Mrs. Hearth gave a huge sigh. "Take some chocolate; it will help." Sara grabbed onto one, but Jake stayed silent and still. "Abigail is afraid, Sara. You cannot blame anyone for their fears."

Sara swallowed the chocolate she'd popped into her mouth whole. "This fear's just stupid. She's prejudice and harsh and cold."

Before anyone could answer, I stepped through the open door, feeling bad for eavesdropping.

"What are we talking about?" I asked as I sat at the table, not looking at the chocolate. I both wanted it and didn't, so the "didn't" won out.

"Mom," Sara spat before Mrs. Hearth could answer, confirming my suspicions. "Mom and her stupid fears and how everyone should just bend to her picture of the world."

Mrs. Hearth took Sara's hand. "What Sara is trying to say, dear, is that Abigail is rather set in her ways, and this can cause problems."

"Like trying to force your kid to give up their problems, or deny them the one person that understands their kind of problems," Sara hissed, pulling her hand from her grandmother's grip.

"Which is all the more reason we should talk to her without Lizzie and Jake here."

I glanced at Jake, having almost forgotten him. He was picking apart a small ball of chocolate, not looking at anyone.

"I should go with 'em, then," Sara said. "It's not like I'm not a problem as well."

"Sara," Mrs. Hearth sighed.

"What? You know it's true."

"I know you and your mother have had some differences, but I thought they were long since in the past?"

"No way. Not with mom. She never forgets these things."

"Either way, I think you should stay. Jake can take Lizzie, and they will be back after dinner. By then, we will have calmed all of this down."

"I don't think that's going to happen, and I don't think you believe so either, grams, but fine. I'll stay and see this blow up in our faces. What's the worst that can happen, right? Mom could split up the coven or something. Good riddance, I say."

"Sara!"

"Fine, sorry. Whatever."

Sara fell back in her chair, crossing her arms and legs and not looking at her grandmother. Jake reached over and squeezed her shoulder, but she wouldn't look at him either. With another sigh, Mrs. Hearth stood and returned to the counter to make preparations for lunch.

Finally, Sara sighed and stood as well, walking over to help her grandmother.

12

"Hey, Jake? Could I speak with you for a moment?" I asked.

"Sure," he answered, leaning forward in his chair.

"Alone?"

Jake opened and closed his mouth once before he nodded and pushed up from the chair. At the counter, Sara turned to glance at us, but she didn't say anything.

Without another word, I led the way out and onto the porch. The cold autumn wind instantly bit through my thin sweater, and I pulled its arms down to cover my fingers. Jake brought both our jackets and helped me into mine before closing the door. I mumbled my thanks and turned to stare across the street.

For a moment, we only stood there, neither looking at the other, before Jake broke the silence. "What can I help you with?"

Drawing a deep breath, I turned to look at him. "You said there was a way to summon ghosts?" He nodded. I drew another breath and wrapped my arms around myself. "If we don't find anything at the church, I want to try and summon mom. She may give us the answers we seek." Jake furrowed his brow and opened his mouth to speak, but I hurried to speak over him. "I know we could summon her now and save the gas-money, but

I don't know if I can face her yet. It's too fresh."

I turned my face away, looking at my childhood home again. Even with the lights on, it looked empty and sad. Or maybe that was just me projecting my feelings onto it.

"I was going to say that it wouldn't be possible," Jake said in a low, soothing voice. I glanced at him, and he nodded before sitting on the porch-banister. "The newly dead are the hardest to summon. We don't know why, but my theory is that it takes them time to get to grips with their new reality, and so they may not be able to hear a summoning, or even know how to answer."

I stared at him for a long time, not sure what to say or even feel. I was relieved I wouldn't be able to see mom right now, but also sad I didn't have the opportunity. It had been a strange comfort I didn't know I needed. Now that it was gone? It felt like I had lost her all over again.

Shaking my head, I turned and sat beside Jake. We both looked through the kitchen window, seeing Sara and Mrs. Hearth working at the counter. Sara was laughing at something the older woman had said. Even Mrs. Hearth had a mischievous twist to her lips.

"We could maybe try your aunt," Jake said after a while. "I'm not sure how it would work with her, but I think we have a better shot at summoning her than your mom." I could feel his gaze at me. "I know you want to know if she's ok."

I wrapped my arms around me again, suddenly shivering from much more than the cold. What if we couldn't summon aunt Ellie? She had been dead for years, yes, but she had only been true-dead less than a day. And what if we couldn't summon her for some other reason? Because of the way I helped her move on? Using necromancy may have hurt her, somehow. Or maybe she had been too hurt by the wendigo already. She had been dying, so maybe she was completely gone now?

My shivering was getting more and more intense, and my teeth were chattering. It was all I could do not to claw at my face to make it stop, to feel anything other than my muscles aching and the empty numbness in my stomach.

"Hey, Lizzie." When I didn't answer, Jake touched my upper arm. His touch was like a shock that shot out from where he made contact and numbed the shakings in that arm. "You didn't do anything wrong."

I sniffled, and he moved his hand to wrap around my shoulders, pulling me against him.

For half a second, I considered pushing away. I hardly knew this man, and he already knew more about me than Mark ever had. And who did this guy think he was to try and comfort me this way? To touch me? But I didn't feel any anger or rage or fear that I would expect from a stranger touching me. Instead, the numbness in my stomach grew a little smaller as gratitude started filling the space.

Jake held me and murmured sweet nothings until my shivers finally stopped. I stayed in his arms a little longer, thankful for the warmth and company. It almost made me snicker, considering I had his girlfriend in my bed every night, and now here he was, hugging me as well. I felt less alone in those moments than I usually did. Even in a house full of witches and people that loved me or cared about me, I felt alone, somehow. I think that was why Sara made a point out of always touching me, of taking every excuse to be close to me. At least that's what I told myself, for I didn't dare hope or think about the alternative. She was in a relationship with this kind and gentle man, and I did not wish to ruin that. Even if I could still taste her on my lips.

"Are you feeling a little better?" Jake asked after a moment.

I nodded and pushed from him, but even as I sat straight, he kept his arm around my shoulders. When I met his eyes, they were narrowed in concern.

"Thank you," I said. "I'm sorry."

"What are you saying sorry for?"

I blushed, glad it was near invisible with my skin. "For, you know..." I waved at the air between us, at my own body, at my face.

Jake shook his head. "Don't ever apologize for feeling." He flashed a grin. "And if you worry about the hug, you can call it a trade, if that makes you feel better. Next time I'm falling apart, you help comfort me, and we're even."

I couldn't help but smile in return. "Fine, I'll do that."

His grin grew and he reached out his free hand. "'tis a deal, then."

As I shook his hand, something moved at the edge of my vision. Jake must have seen it as well, for he turned just at the same moment. Still holding each other's hands, we stared as a white dove hopped up the driveway, eyes fixed on us. I had half a second to remember Elizabeth's words about a white dove being Jesus's soul, before the air seemed pulled from my lungs and all the color was leeched from the world. It seemed to swirl toward the dove, who almost shone in the suddenly grey and gloomy surroundings. Then the sound and air and colors rushed back out, and a woman stood in the dove's place.

It took less than two seconds for it all to happen, but it seemed to stop my brain from functioning properly.

The woman walked forward, saying something in a language I couldn't understand but made Jake's hand tighten in mine.

Then my mind stuttered to life again, and I noticed that the woman standing in Mrs. Hearth's driveway, in view of the whole neighborhood, was completely naked.

Her eyes were piercing blue and holding mine, and I wasn't able to look away. She was tall, almost taller than me, and blond. Her hair hanging thick and wavy to her waist, and her body was strong, with broad shoulders and hips. She seemed to be all lean muscle and curves. Like the perfect woman.

"Ich kann Ihnen helfen, das zu finden, wonach Sie suchen," the woman said and stepped closer.

"Huh?" I answered, not understanding a word.

"That's German," Jake said, pulling his hand from mine.

"You know it?" I asked.

"Vetrau mir," the woman said before Jake could answer.

"Nein," he answered.

"Huh?"

The woman narrowed her eyes at him for a moment before spitting out a long line of words I didn't have a chance of following.

"What's she saying?" I asked Jake when the woman stopped talking.

Jake was staring at her, mouth open, but at my words he shook his head and started pulling off his jacket. "She claims to be a Salige Fräulein. *Bitte fassen Sie diese an,"* he said as he hurried down the porch steps.

I bit back another ''huh''. "A what now?" Yeah, for that sounds so much smarter!

The woman took the jacket and shrugged into it, thankfully hiding her boobs.

"I honestly don't know," Jake answered, blinking at the woman. "But she said she was from the Spirit World, and she's here to help you."

"Well, bring her inside, then," Mrs. Hearth said from the doorway, making both Jake and me jump. "Lunch is ready."

The woman just inclined her head at Mrs. Hearth, as if they knew each other.

Jake managed to talk Gudrun into drying up and putting on clothes before lunch, which proved not as easy as one would think. She was as tall as me but as shapely as Sara, so in the end, she borrowed a dress from Mrs. Hearth and a cardigan from me. The dress was a little too short, but it fit everything else because it was so shapeless, while the cardigan was too tight to close across the chest, but at least she was dressed.

"I have been thinking about using it for new handkerchiefs," Mrs. Hearth confessed as we all sat down to eat. "It is not becoming on anyone, to be honest, but at least the blue matches her eyes."

Lunch was a homemade vegetarian stew with homemade bread and jam at the side. I managed to eat almost half the bowl of food but didn't touch the bread. Everyone but the woman glowered at me when I didn't eat anything else, but none of them pushed for me to eat more.

After the first round, Mrs. Hearth prompted Jake to get the woman to talk. For half a second, she stared at all of us like we were unruly children, before she sighed and started talking. In-between bites and questions, Jake worked as translator.

"My name is Gudrun," the blond woman said. "I'm a Salige Fräulein."

"And what is that?" Sara asked.

Gudrun and Jake talked a lot back and forth, Jake with a perplexed look on his face, before he finally answered. "A white woman. She claims to be a spirit creature from Germany who helps people and the world."

"And how did she end up here?" Mrs. Hearth asked.

This time, Jake translated without questions. "I lived in the Spirit World with my sisters for a long time after the Banishment. We were happy there, but soon we fell into slumber. Everyone fell asleep. After a long sleep, longer than anyone can know, we woke. The world was shaking and burning. Life was sucked out of our world. When life was almost gone, the world stilled. Something had changed. A breeze ran through the world, telling us that the Veil had been broken. All of us knew that our world needed time to heal. Me and my sisters left our home to come here, so as not to put more strain on our own world."

"When was this?"

"Not long ago. We traveled for some time, we were far from the Rift but we fly fast, and then we were in the Grey World for a while. There is no time there, so I don't know how long."

"How long have you been in our world, then?"

"Three days."

"And what have you been doing during those days?"

At this, Gudrun pointed her bread at me. "Watching."

Everyone turned to me.

"Why?" I asked when I found my voice again. "I haven't seen you. My ghosts haven't seen you. How can you have been watching me?"

She shook her head. "You have seen me. You all have, but not like this."

"How, then?"

She blinked at me for a second before standing, and slipped out of the dress and jacket, standing naked before us. Jake turned his face away, blushing, but Sara looked on with interest. One second Gudrun stood in front of us before a flash of light blinded us, and a white dove fluttered its wings and flew up, landing on the back of the chair where Gudrun had sat a moment before.

I gaped. The others gaped.

I was the first to find my voice. "You were the bird at the funeral. You were the one I saw yesterday." The dove cocked its head, clearly not understanding, and I kicked Jake under the table. "Translate."

We'd seen her change from dove to human outside, but somehow the connection didn't click into place before seeing it again. I blamed the shock.

Jake stammered for a second before he did as asked.

The bird nodded before flying down to the floor again, where she changed back and put on her clothes. We sat in silence until she was back at the table.

"That still doesn't answer why you've been watching me, and what about these sisters you were talking about? And why help now? Why not three days ago?"

"I was not able to transform into human form until now. And my sisters have been looking for others like you. Humans that can help us."

"Help you with what?" Sara asked, her voice suddenly defensive.

Warmth blossomed in my heart hearing her voice, but I

tampered it down.

"All these creatures weren't supposed to leave the Spirit World at once. It has made the energy loud and it's our job to help it calm down again."

Jake furrowed his brow. "I have no idea what she's talking about."

"I think I do," Mrs. Hearth said and started gathering the plates.

"What, then?" Sara asked.

Mrs. Hearth put the plates on the counter before she answered. "It was her translated name that made me think of it. I think she is one of the creatures that are pure magic. Their job is to make sure the world's magic is in balance."

"How?" I asked.

She put the pot of stew in the fridge and wrapped the leftover bread in a towel before putting it in the breadbox. By the time she was done, it felt like I was vibrating with anticipation.

Finally, Mrs. Hearth sat down again. "The world is made of energy. Everything alive is made of energy and have a thread connected to that energy. We need it to survive. Spirits are connected to the energy of their own world, but they are also connected to the energy of this one. That is why we can see them. Because they are of this world. There exist creatures, both human and spirits, that does not have that link. They are full of the energy and created purely of the energy of the world, and their job is to make sure it stay balanced."

"How?" I asked, glancing at the others. Jake was translating to Gudrun in a low voice, but Sara was looking bored, like she'd heard it all before. Maybe she had. Maybe this was witch knowledge one-o-one.

"That I do not know. I am not one of these creatures. They

are often referred to as white spirits, or white women and men, and exists outside of time. These Salige Fräulein may be one of those creatures."

"How do we know she isn't lying?" Sara asked. "How do we know she's what she says she is and not just some random evil demon?"

"We don't, dear."

Sara opened and closed her mouth a few times before she shrugged. "Neat."

Mrs. Hearth smiled at her granddaughter. "I think all we can do is let her explain why she thinks dear Lizzie can help her, and then do our best."

"She said she could help us as well," Jake said. "She said she could help Lizzie find what she's looking for."

Mrs. Hearth's smile grew even wider. "Ask her then."

Jake furrowed his brow before asking. Gudrun answered easily enough. Jake's expression changed to wonder then worry before his face calmed again. Gudrun, having seen this as she spoke, laughed a warm laugh and patted his cheek before saying something. Sara made a grimace at me, and I smiled, but my smile died as Jake turned back to me.

"She's saying you're the reason the Rift happened in the first place. You destroyed the Veil and let all those spirits out. When you left the Grey World, you left a piece of yourself behind, and brought a piece of that world with you. As a shaman, you already had a root in our world and the Spirit World. After your death, you also have a root in the Grey World. That is why you can control every spirit that pass through it."

A silence fell and I looked around the room. Mrs. Hearth had one hand clutching at her chest, her face pale. Sara, Jake, and Gudrun were all staring at me. Elizabeth and Eleanor were standing by the window, having looked outside but now turned to Gudrun with worry and wonder on their faces. Somewhere in the house, I heard Johana scream with laughter.

"Ok, and what does that mean?" I asked when I couldn't take their looks any more.

Jake glanced at Gudrun before he answered: "She say's you owe the world, now. That you have a job to do, just like her."

"And that job is?"

"To right the wrong. To fix the world."

14

What Gudrun had said resonated with me. I knew some things needed fixing, and a part of me thought that it was my responsibility. It wasn't anything I hadn't thought before, but it kept getting more and more real each time someone said something to the effect, and the more real it got, the heavier it got. I could almost feel it crushing down on my shoulders, making it hard to breathe and concentrate on anything at all.

It was a relief when we finally left the table. I needed to feel like I was doing something, and going to find a shaman was a good start.

I hurried to my bedroom to change into something more fitting for a road trip. It was strange, but I had never liked leaving the house without looking at least decent, and I wanted to impress the shaman if we found him.

I'd left the door ajar as I entered, and my fright of ghosts seemed to take that as an invitation to join me there.

I stopped folding my pajama-bottoms and looked at them.

"What's up?" I asked, not sure what was going on. I could feel worry through the threads connecting us. But it wasn't worrying for me as much as over the whole situation. And there was eagerness there too, and stubbornness, although I couldn't tell who felt what.

It was strange knowing that much about what the group felt in general.

"Will you make us stay behind?" Magdalena said, surprising me. I so seldom heard her speak; it was easy to forget she was there.

"No," I said before I had time to consider it.

"Are you certain? For you did so earlier today."

"Yes, I did." I squatted, so I was eye-to-eye with her. "But that was because I was afraid for you. Who knows what might have happened if you came with me to battle the wendigo." Magdalena squeezed a little closer to Eleanor, but she met my eyes stubbornly. "Leaving you behind now would have the opposite effect."

The six-year-old nodded. "Good."

I smothered a smile. She was so serious; it wouldn't do to ruin it by calling her cute. With a groan, I pushed to my feet.

"You will not be going to the church?" Eleanor asked.

I started folding the bottoms again. "No. Gudrun said the shaman was North, so we're skipping the church all-together. It should save us some time. Maybe I will be able to learn something that can help. Finally." The last was said as much to myself as to them.

Something vibrated through the threads, but I couldn't discern what it was. When I looked at the ghosts, they were exchanging glances, before Elizabeth stepped forward.

"Was your mom Christian?" she asked, lifting her chin a little.

My hands froze. "No," I answered, meeting her eyes. "She always respected the faith, though, probably as a result of being left at that church, but she never really much believed in anything."

"Why not?"

I started folding again. "She once told me that she couldn't believe in an entity that would bring about so much suffering as was in the world today."

"Maybe that is why you have the Sight." she spat. "As punishment."

I looked at her again, unsure of how to react to that. Where was this coming from?

"What about you?" Eleanor asked. "Are you a Christian?"

"No," I said, answering both of them. "The Sight is something I inherited through blood, not because I don't believe in some old white man sitting in the sky and punishing people even before they're born." Elizabeth clenched her jaw and stared daggers at me. I continued: "And no, I'm not Christian. Connor was, and we went to church with him for Christmas and such, but mom and I didn't really believe any of it."

"Then what do you believe?" Elizabeth asked, her voice hard.

"I believe in ghosts and energy and life," I answered, forcing a smile.

"What about *l'âme*?" Eleanor asked.

I stared at her, taking a moment to remember what the word meant, then it clicked. I suddenly realized why Elizabeth was so adamant in her belief in Christ and God. For weren't they souls stuck here on earth? Not able to move on? I understood their need to believe in a Heaven or Hell when all this was over, for if not that, what was there for them when moving on? Just the Grey World?

"I believe in the soul," I said. "Or at least something resembling it." Elizabeth relaxed a little. "But can I ask why you are wondering this now?"

The two oldest ghosts exchanged glances again, and I felt

their reprehension through the threads between us.

"Jonathan, Johana," I said, turning to the twins. They were sitting on my bed, making grimaces at Magdalena, who scowled back, just as serious as before. At my voice, all three turned to look at me. "Why don't you take Magdalena and make sure all the other ghosts are safe over at Key-house before we leave?"

The twins groaned, but Elizabeth glared, and they pushed off the bed. Taking one of Magdalena's hands each, they headed for the door.

"We'll meet you by the car," I said. "You can sit on the roof again."

That put a spring in their step.

The three of us watched them go before Eleanor and Elizabeth turned back to me.

"What is this about? Why are you wondering about this now?" I asked, finally finishing with the pajama-bottoms.

"Just what that...creature said," Eleanor answered. "About what she is, and what the other spirits are."

"And there is what the witches have said," Elizabeth chimed in. "About how their magic works and how the world works." She was staring at her hands, folded primly in front of her. "What if we are not truly who we believe? Just shadows left behind when our bodies died?"

"No," I answered. "I don't believe that. I can't. Not after what happened to me. To you. I must believe there is some sort of rest, some sort of price when this is all over. Even just a good, deep sleep would be enough for me, but there must be something. It can't just all be wandering around on this earth forever."

Elizabeth looked up and met my eyes. "Are you certain? For that dove we saw yesterday was truly not Christ's soul if it was

Ms. Gudrun. And if that was not Christ, then who is to tell if he and God are even real?"

I blinked at her. A ghost was having a crisis-of-faith. I wasn't sure what that made me feel. Sad, mostly. And tired. Like there was always another thing coming. No rest. It never ended. It made the burden of what I had to fix seem even heavier, and I wanted to collapse onto the bed and sleep and sleep and sleep.

Eleanor was saying something in French that I didn't catch, but when she stopped speaking, I continued: "God is what you believe him to be, I think. I may not believe in the wise, all-knowing man watching over us, believing all women are sinners from birth and punishing them, but I understand those that do, those that need to. And I believe everyone has their own picture and idea of God, and that is the God they know."

I sat down on the bed, folding my hands in my lap to match Elizabeth. She was still looking at me, tears in her eyes.

Steps sounded in the hall, and someone knocked at the door. Jake pushed it open just enough to see me sitting on the bed.

"You ok?" he asked.

"Yes," I said, standing. "I was just talking with my ghosts. They had... questions."

"Can I help?"

I glanced at Eleanor and Elizabeth, but they both shook their heads, and Eleanor wrapped her arms around Elizabeth.

"No," I answered, struggling to see Jake through their bodies. They were almost corporeal, but if I focused, I could see through them. "We're good."

He nodded. "Ready to go?"

After another glance at the two ghosts, I nodded and walked past them.

15

Outside, it had started raining, which made me even happier to be doing something other than just sitting inside, waiting for something to happen.

As we left Sky Harbour, it became clear Gudrun only knew in what direction the shaman was. She couldn't pinpoint him, but she would point us in the right direction or tell when we were far off course. I was not looking forward to the drive; having to sit still did not fit into my new restlessness. Who knew how long it would take?

We'd left just before four o'clock, and Jake was keeping his conversation with Gudrun going. I kept out of it until the news came on, and when I turned it up, they both quieted down.

I listened with only half an ear as the newswoman talked about events from around the world. A volcano on Iceland had acted up and was still smoking, and air-traffic had been canceled for almost two weeks now. And they were still trying to count all the dead after a tsunami that hit Thailand.

Finally, the newswoman focused on Canada. A snow-storm had appeared out of no-where in the Rockies, and a team of tourists was still missing. Then she turned to Nova Scotia and talked about a trail of bodies left behind from Sky Harbour and toward Lower Woods Harbour, before following the coastline back up again.

"Some are wondering if these killers are the same as the Dog Hunter, whom for just over a week now have been killing dogs along the same route," the woman said before moving on to another story.

"The stream of missing people plaguing this island took an ugly turn this morning when the body of Philip Hammond, a twenty-six-year-old father from Sky Harbour, was found. Philip went missing just yesterday when out for an evening walk. There was hope he would turn up, having just wandered off like some of the other missing person reports over the last week. At half-past-six this morning, that hope was crushed as a pedestrian found his body. The police have so far not given out much detail about his death, but they do believe it to be foul play."

I turned down the radio again and focused on the road, still listening but only with half an ear. Something was tickling at the back of my mind.

I didn't know what it was, so I tried to focus on the rest of the news. It was much of the same.

"And this is only one of many disturbing news coming from Sky Harbour lately. The police have gotten reports of children spotted in the woods, people being stalked as they walk home at night, others sure that someone has broken into their homes at night but never finding any proof of this, and even a few cases of people swearing they have seen people moving around at the local graveyard. When we asked the police about this, they said they thought it was some kids playing Halloween pranks on the town, but not everyone is so sure. We have Dr. Ingskiss from the local hospital here with us today, and you think there might be more to all of these events than just some teenagers?"

"Yes," a man answered over the radio. "I think there might be a kind of sleep epidemic going around."

"Why do you think that?" the woman asked.

"Because people have been flooding their doctor's offices after sleep terrors, sleep paralysis, or not sleeping at all. Usually, this might just be a sign of the times, but they all say it started around the same time, around a week ago. Many of them also talk about hallucinations, and many of these are similar."

"And so the major of Sky Harbour has asked the Department of Health to send someone. According to our sources at the office, a representative is indeed on their way to the small town to test both water and air. What they expect to find, they have yet to reveal."

They continued to the weather, and Jake turned down the volume.

"Those things are all because of this Veil thing, aren't they? And the damage I did when beating the Red Woman?" I asked, looking at him.

He was chewing on his lower lip but stopped at my voice before giving a slight nod. "I think so."

"So what can we do? Those people being killed. What could do that?"

"Many things. Without more information, I can't put my finger on one specific creature doing it. Maybe there are many different killers?"

"But why go toward Lower Woods? What's there?"

He shrugged. "It's South. Maybe they want to get somewhere warmer?"

"Why be here in the first place, then?"

"Maybe they didn't have a choice? I don't know, Lizzie. I know as much as you do at this point, but that's why we're here, isn't it? To get answers?"

As he said it, he turned to look at Gudrun. I glanced in the rearview mirror, meeting her blue gaze for a second before turning my eyes back to the road.

"Let me know if she knows anything," I said dryly.

In the end, she did know something. Yes, most of those happenings were because of spirits that had come through the rift I created in the Veil. While there were other holes and rift, the one I created was by far the biggest, and it was through that most of them had escaped, arriving in Canada. Thanks to me.

With everything that had happened so far today, I was going numb, and grateful for it.

Jake paused his chatting to answer his phone. It had been making a kind of ''waho''-sound since just after the news ended.

"So, what is this Veil you all keep talking about?" I asked when he put his phone away.

"The Veil is a barrier," Jake answered after a quick word to Gudrun, probably to translate what I had said. "It was raised hundreds of years ago by magic-users across the globe. As it was created, it sucked all spirit-creatures back to their own world. The Veil has kept us safe from things like the wendigo for generations. Every Samhain, all witches come together to strengthen the Veil. I don't know about other magic-users, but I can only imagine they have their own rituals and the like to keep it strong. None of us want the things captured there to return."

"What about the Grey World? The place where I was when I died?" I asked.

"That we actually don't know. We didn't create it."

"Maybe she knows," I said, nodding my head backward to

indicate Gudrun.

"Want me to ask?"

"Why not? We have the time."

Jake nodded and turned, speaking hurriedly in German. The more he spoke, the more secure he seemed to get in the language, and I wondered how it was to remember so well. I'd taken French in school, and while I didn't remember anything at the top of my head, speaking with Eleanor and understanding some of her French made it clear the knowledge was still there. Maybe I should ask Eleanor and Jake to help me get better at it? I could have used it a time or two at work, and I'd always wanted to visit Paris. Speaking the language could hardly hurt.

"So, uhm, Gudrun has a lot to say about the Veil. And other things." Jake said after Gudrun had talked for a long, good while. Even not knowing the language, I recognized the anger in her voice.

"I heard," I said.

Jake cleared his throat a few times, checked his phone, then started translating. "The Veil didn't take every spirit-creature; only those with more spirit-blood than man-blood. All the magic-users in today's world are descendants of spirits and humans coupling. Some of the magic-users that have gone extinct in this world did so because of the Veil. It considered them more spirit than human and grabbed at them. But humans would not survive in the Spirit World, so the magic split. It created the Grey World, a place between the Human World and the Spirit World, where the mutts were kept. But unlike the Spirit World, the Grey World wasn't created with life in mind. Instead, it lulled all those who stayed there into a deep sleep, and so they stayed frozen in time, waiting for the day when the Veil was broken, and they could return to their own world."

"We did not sleep," Eleanor said, talking over Jake's next words. I glanced at her in the rearview mirror, for a moment surprised that I was able to see all the ghosts in the back seat, then I returned my attention to the conversation. When Jake drew a breath, I mentioned what Eleanor had said.

After yet another small conversation in German, Jake answered. "I think that's because they were all dead. They were already frozen as they were, so why would the world freeze them again?"

"Makes sense, I guess. But what about the Spirit World? Gudrun said they were sleeping when the Rift happened. Why?"

"Because the Veil is getting weaker," Jake translated. "Because smaller rifts and openings have appeared, and so the magic of the Grey World has seeped into ours, lulling us into hibernation. Just like those trapped in the Grey World, we have been waiting."

"What kind of... people slept in the Grey World?"

"The shapeshifters, the ocean people, the elementals, and their many children. My sisters and I were supposed to be there as well, but because of our job, we were able to cross into the Spirit World and live there."

Jake furrowed his brow as he said this before he turned and spoke in a hushed, hurried voice.

"What?" I asked after Gudrun answered, but Jake lifted a hand to silence me and asked another question. I glowered at the rain-slicked road ahead.

"He said only dark spirits, those that were a danger to humans, were captured by the Veil," Eleanor said, surprising me into glancing at her again, and Gudrun into silence for a moment.

"You know German?" I asked at the same time as Gudrun

grinned and twirled one of Eleanor's long wheat-blond locks between her fingers, crooning her next words. Jake looked between Gudrun and me but didn't say anything.

"Yes," Eleanor said, swatting Gudrun's hand away from her hair. "My *Grand-mère* was German, and she made sure we knew the language, even if I had hoped never to use it."

"Why? And how come she can touch you?"

"She is a spirit, *non?* We can touch each other." Eleanor was scowling now. "And I do not trust the Germans."

"Why?"

She met my eyes in the mirror. "I am allowed some privacy, *non?*"

I looked back on the road. "Of course. Sorry."

Eleanor nodded and turned to look out the window, absent-mindedly stroking Magdalena's hair. The girl was sitting in Elizabeth's lap in the middle seat.

"Mr. Jake claimed that the Veil only imprisoned evil spirit-creatures, but Ms. Gudrun said otherwise. She said that the Veil took everyone, good or bad, and it is one of the reasons this world has fallen into decline. The magic did not discriminate. The only ones not affected were those that cast the spell to create it in the first place."

"So witches and shamans?" I asked.

"And all the other magic-users of the world," Jake said when Gudrun had translated Eleanor's words.

"What kind? How many magic-users are there?" I asked.

"Many. The tradition we witches follow is mainly middle and northern European, and we are the most numerous magic-users in North America. There is a multitude of shaman sub-types based on where in the world the shaman comes from and what tradition is in their blood. Their type of magic differs accordingly. There are also many sub-types of witches. Like the rune-witches from Scandinavia have their own traditions and powers that in some ways seem shamanic, although they are closer to us witches than shamans."

"What about a male-dominated type? Like with witches being almost all female?"

"The closest are magicians," Jake answered. "But we don't know if they only breed boys, or if the power is only inherited by boys, or if the powers appear randomly and the magicians only chose to train boys."

"Why not?"

"Like the shamans, they keep to themselves, and we never had a lot of them here in Canada or America. They were popular in the European courts before most of the royal families were dethroned, so they stayed there."

"So, if you had to guess, how many different... did you call it classes? No, traditions. How many different traditions do you think there are?"

Jake stared out the window for a little while. I was about to ask again when my phone rang.

"Could you see who it is?" I asked, but Jake was already reaching for the center console.

"Unknown number," he said after a quick glance at the screen.

"Let it go to voicemail."

"You sure?"

"Yes. I really don't like speaking on the phone while I drive. If it's important, they'll leave a message."

The phone rang and rang until it finally stopped. Shortly after, a message pinged in. Jake was still holding the phone, and I gave him my code so he could log in and see what it said.

"They left a voicemail," Jake said, staring at the phone.

"Figured they would."

"You want to listen to it now?"

"No. I'll do it when we stop for gas. Is it ok if we do it soon?"

"Sure."

He put the phone away. "As to how many types of magic-users there are in the world, I don't know. Probably in the hundreds. Unfortunately, we witches have gotten a little elitist. It's one of the things Sara and I hope to change."

I nodded, and the car fell into silence for a mile or two. I could hear the twins laughing from the roof every now and again, but that was about it.

"How does she know where the shaman is?" I asked after we drove by another off-ramp. I'd considered following it to fill gas, but figured we were good until the next station showed up.

"Apparently, shaman magic stands out somehow," Jake translated. "Both shamans and witches with the sight have roots in the Spirit World and our own world, but the root of the shamans goes much deeper. Because of that, spirits like Gudrun can sense shamans."

"If there are so many magic-users out there, how does she know who's what?"

"We feel differently, somehow, but also the same. She can tell if someone is the same type, and so she knows to pair you up with someone that has the same signature," Jake said.

I wanted to ask more, but Jake and Gudrun were talking again, so I tuned them out and thought about what might meet me at the end of this drive. Hopefully, answers to all my questions, but I feared there would be more judgment, like with Abigail. What if the shamans hated necromancers as much as the witches? What if the shaman we found would try to kill me on sight? A week ago, that thought would have made me afraid, but now I almost didn't care. It felt like everything was happening around me, and all I could do was stand back and watch. If I tried to step into the maelstrom of events, I was sure all my bottled up feelings would tear me apart, but right now, it was just stuff passing me by. A glimpse of fear or sorrow or rage, then it was gone.

16

The further North we drove, the colder it became. The rain turned to sleet, which made it somewhat easier to see, but made the world seem asleep. It reminded me of the Grey World, and I shuddered.

When the next off-ramp came into view, I signaled and got on it.

Just off the freeway was a gas station, and I found a reclusive spot and parked. Handing the keys to Jake, I stepped out of the car, grabbing my phone on the way.

Jake met me outside. "You want me to fill it and drive from now on?"

"Fill up, yes, drive from now on, I really don't know?"

He nodded before he stuck his head into the car and said something to Gudrun.

I turned and walked away.

The gas station lay on a small hill overlooking the freeway on one side and with a tired forest at its back. I headed toward the small green area beside the station proper and leaned against the wall, just under the roof as to not get wet, and turned my back to the road and the cars to look at the woods as I found the voicemail.

"Hello. I hope I have reached Elizabeth Key. My name is Melania

Bell, and I'm a detective with the Halifax Police Department. Me and my partner, Henrik Vandom, would like to ask you some questions at your earliest convenience about your father."

She followed up by informing me that they were at this point not investigating me, but just wanted my statement on a few things to get a better picture of the situation. After that, she gave me her number, then made a joke about how I probably didn't need it because of caller-ID and hung up. The joke sounded old and over-used, like she said it every time she left a message like this.

What the situation was, she didn't say. Sky Harbour didn't have its own police station. We had an office with two holding cells and a few local cops, but nothing as serious as detectives.

I stared at my phone for a long while. I wasn't feeling numb anymore. I'd stepped into the maelstrom, and as I'd feared, the feelings were hitting me hard. There was the fear of what I was about to do and the unknown of my situation and of what the police might want. There was the sorrow for mom's death, and Connor's oppression, and the loss of aunt Ellie and Sanderson, and Abigail's betrayal. And there was anger over the betrayal, and anger over mom having to die for me to come into my powers. Some of that was rage at the Red Woman. She was dead and gone, and still I was so angry at her; it felt like my chest was being ripped open by red hot blades. There was some relief there as well. Relief that mom didn't have to suffer anymore, and relief that we had captured the wendigo and that we were finally doing something and maybe I could fix everything soon. There was hope that things could return to normal, and confusion over what the future might hold. Much of that confusion was born from Sara and her kiss. And all those feelings hit me again and again until I could hardly breathe.

I doubled over and closed my eyes, trying to breathe the way I'd done the few times I tried yoga. At first, it didn't feel like anything was happening, and I wanted to lash out. It didn't matter at what or who, but something. I stayed with the breathing, however, and soon the pressure in my head and chest seemed to lessen. A few tears escaped my closed eyes, but my breathing was better, and the maelstrom was growing smaller and smaller until I could step out of it. It was a relief when the numbness crept back.

I sighed and opened my eyes, looking at the rain coming down for a few seconds before pocketing my phone and starting around the building again.

Jake had driven the car to the other side of the building after filling the tank, and I could see both him and Gudrun sitting in it, Jake talking and gesticulating.

A scream stopped me in my tracks, and I spun around, looking through the windows and into the kiosk A woman lay crumpled on the floor, clutching her bleeding stomach. The teenager behind the register stood with his arms in the air, crying, as a man waved a knife around.

I took a step back, about to reach for my phone to call the police, when I noticed the others inside. The same kid was standing by the toilets, cleaning the floor with a bored look on his face and glancing toward the three men seated on the other side of the room, drinking coffee and talking.

In the corner of my eye, I saw my ghosts flying toward me, worry and fear on their faces. They must have sensed my distress through our threads.

My eyes flew back to the scene just as the man with the knife turned and ran toward me. I flung myself back as he lifted his arm to open the door, but the moment he touched it, he dissolved into smoke. Behind him, the kid flew to the woman's side, but she was lying still now.

"Can you help me?" someone asked beside me.

I screamed and spun around.

A woman stood there, looking at me with pleading eyes. I stared at her for a second before turning to look inside again, but the scene was gone.

"Can you help me?" she asked again.

My hands were shaking as I turned back to the woman I'd just seen die inside the store. My own ghosts were circling her, and she looked between them and me, a new fear on her face.

"Lizzie?" Jake and Gudrun had stepped out of the car and stood in the rain, looking in my direction. Gudrun, however, wasn't looking at me but at the new ghost. I was sure that's what she was. A ghost. The ghost of the woman I'd just seen murdered.

I lifted a hand, indicating for them to wait and that I was ok, and turned back to the woman.

"I don't know," I said in a hushed tone. "But I hope to find out today. Maybe you could come with us? Or go to my place?"

She was shaking her head, tears filling her eyes. "I can't leave."

"Hey, lady? You alright?"

I spun around at the voice. The three men that had been drinking coffee inside the kiosk stood in the door, looking at me. They must have heard my scream.

"Yes, I just really scared myself, I'm sorry," I answered, almost laughing but able to keep it down. I'd never been a good liar.

"How can you scare yourself?" The teen asked.

"Do you know how cold rain can be down the back of your

jacket?" I snapped back, getting inspiration from the drop just then escaping my hair and trickling down my spine. "And it can really take you by surprise, I tell you. I'm sorry."

The men looked at each other before they looked toward Jake and Gudrun standing by the car. One of the men narrowed his eyes and walked past his buddies and toward me. By the car, Jake started moving as well, but the man reached me first.

"Is he hurting you?" The man asked in a low voice. "Just blink twice for yes, and we'll help you."

My heart filled for this stranger, but I shook my head and managed a smile. "No, he's not, but thank you."

"You sure?" he asked, his eyes jumping between mine, as if to look for a lie or any hint that I was going to blink.

"Yes, I'm sure. But really, thank you."

He stood still for a moment before nodding. "If you say so."

Jake reached us. "Lizzie, what's going on? You ok?"

"Yes," I said, forcing a laugh.

"She screamed because a drop trickled down her back," the teen said.

I glared at him. "I'm really sorry to have startled you all. Really, I am, and really, thank you." I said to the man. He was looking between Jake and me, and somehow seemed to decide that he could trust my word, for he gave a smile and a nod.

"Sorry for bothering you, then." He winked, turned, and walked back to his buddies, ushering them inside.

I sagged a little.

"What really happened?" Jake asked, looking after the men.

"A ghost. Both a memory and an actual one." I turned back to the woman, but she was gone. "Where did she go?" I asked, looking at my own ghosts.

Before they could answer, someone screamed behind me. I

spun to see the scene inside the kiosk unfolding again.

"What?" Jake asked.

I sighed, feeling like a weight lay on my shoulders, pushing me down into the earth and through. I was the only one that could help this woman not re-live her murder, but I had no idea how.

"I'll tell you in the car," I finally said as the killer ran toward the door.

The woman didn't appear this time, and I looked on as the kid called someone on his phone and tried to stop the blood flowing from the woman's stomach.

As I climbed into the passenger seat of the car, I promised myself to be back and help her. The sooner, the better.

17

Safely back in the car, I told Jake who had called and what they said.

"Your stepmom probably called him in missing earlier today. Last she knew, he was coming to speak to you, after all," Jake answered, staring at his phone.

"Did you know?" I asked.

"That the police showed up? Yes. Sara has been messaging me with regular updates of the dinner and what else is going on there."

As if on cue, his phone made the "waho" sound again.

I shrugged. "What I can't understand is why they called in detectives for just one missing man! I know he's got money and is a middle-aged white dude, but still. One disappearance shouldn't warrant detectives in Sky Harbour."

"'tis not just him, though," Jake answered. "You heard the news. There is a multitude of things going on in your hometown, and the regular humans were bound to notice sooner or later."

"Guess it was sooner," I said and buried my face in my hands. "What are we going to do? They must have seen his car in our driveway. How will we explain that?"

"Thankfully, we have some time to think it over," Jake said and started the car. He was in the driver's seat now. "We are too far from Sky Harbour for it to be any point in turning back, and they left that message almost an hour ago. Might as well continue on our current course and deal with the police tomorrow."

I glanced at him through my fingers. "You really think that is best?"

"I don't think there's any point in doing anything else, to be honest."

Pulling my face from my hands, I brushed my damp hair out of the way and gave a firm nod. "Ok, then. To the shaman we go."

Jake chuckled. "You just sounded like Sara."

A smirk played across my lips. "Well, we did grow up together."

Jake smiled and turned onto the freeway again.

In the back, Eleanor and Elizabeth were talking in low voices about the ghost at the gas station, and how they were glad they weren't stuck. They might be bound to me, but at least they didn't have to relive their death again and again.

Magdalena was sitting in Eleanor's lap – as much as she could without merging with the big, pregnant belly – and looked out the window with wide eyes, silently counting the raindrops running down the glass. The wonder in her eyes it made me think about everything she must have been through since she died. All the things she must have seen and felt. It made me sad, and I wanted to help her with all my heart. Wanted to help all of them.

On the roof, the twins were playing a game of patty-cake. I couldn't hear their voices or the slap of their hands, but I knew anyway.

"Magdalena," I said, turning to meet the ghost's eyes. "Why

don't you go up onto the roof and play with the twins? I'm sure they would appreciate it."

The six-year-old ghost stared at me like I'd grown an extra head.

"That is not a bad idea," Eleanor said. "And you could use the fresh air."

Magdalena looked between the two of us, her eyes narrowing in suspicion, but after a mumbled ok, she let Elizabeth lift her up through the roof. I felt the burst of joy from the twins when they realized she would be joining them, and smiled.

While I'd listened to the message from the police, Jake had bought some food at the gas station, which we ate in silence. Gudrun apparently loved the idea of hotdogs, and she snorted soda out her nose the first time she tasted it, un-used to the carbonates. After that, she giggled every time she took a sip.

Jake cleared his throat after a while. "About Sara."

"What about her?" I asked when he didn't continue.

"Do you know what she and Mrs. Hearth were talking about? Before you asked me to talk and everything with Gudrun happened"

"Sara's powers being corrupt?"

"That, and me."

I turned to look at him. "You? Why?"

His hands clenched around the steering wheel, but his face was as relaxed as ever. "I told you how most witches don't take kindly to chroniclers. How for a long time we were killed as newborns." I nodded when he glanced my way. "Some witches don't believe that anymore, most of the newer generations and some of the older, like Mrs. Hearth. They believe us to be just as human as any other witch, and just as important. Some don't agree, though, and Abigail is one of them. Sara and I have been dating for a long time now, we even live together, but until a few days ago, I never met her mother. I've met Emma and her husband and Mrs. Hearth, but never Abigail. I guess I know why with the reaction she had to me."

"What kind of reaction?"

"First, she didn't know what I was. She kept talking to Sara about how there was a family thing going on and she shouldn't have brought me, for most of the night until Sara finally cracked and told her what I am. I think Abigail almost fainted at the news. Mrs. Hearth brought her a cup of tea and used some of her magic on her. But Abigail snapped and started yelling at Sara about how she had always done what she could to break up the coven, that she was selfish, and did she have any idea what the other witches would think of a witch and a chronicler living together," he had to take a deep breath after the tirade. "She said a few words I would rather not repeat about both Sara and my kind in general before storming out."

"But she didn't seem to mind you all that much after I came over?"

"No, I think Mrs. Hearth has been using her magic on her to keep her calm, but it still doesn't erase all the things she said. She thinks my kind should be drowned at birth, that we weaken the magic in the different bloodlines that spawn us." He spat the last few words.

"She didn't say that, did she?"

"What part?"

"Well, all of it. I know she can be a bit strict, but I can't believe
—"

Jake cut me off, anger in his voice. "I don't know why Abigail or the witches fear a chronicler and a witch being together, but they do, and Abigail thought Sara was only with me because of it. She thought Sara was chasing power."

"Is she?" I asked after a few seconds of thinking.

"No."

"So why is Abigail afraid of it? Is it because of her luck?"

"Yes. She always thought Sara was corrupt, that she was after power and power alone. She even blames Sara for the divorce between her and her husband."

"Sara really loves her dad!"

"I know, but Abigail doesn't. She has decided that Sara is evil. Being together with a chronicler only cemented that belief. We're two bad folks, after all."

"No, you're not."

He smiled a half-smile that didn't reach his eyes.

I leaned back in my own seat and stared straight ahead as well, thinking. Jake's hand on my arm made me aware that I was chewing my nails again, and I hurriedly sat on them. Giving him a grateful smile, I returned to my thoughts.

18

Shortly after, Gudrun led us off the freeway and onto back roads. Amazingly, we only took five wrong turns as we neared the end of our journey, but the only reason we didn't take more was that Jake guessed our destination as we drew near it: Potlotek First Nation.

I had no idea what to expect. Despite my blood and mom's history of trying to find her parents, I'd never been to a reservation before. As we drew closer, I even felt a little resentment toward the people living there. They had all the answers I needed, I was sure, so why couldn't one of them be a shaman and let me live my life? Why did it have to be me? Ok, maybe the resentment was more personal than toward the people at Potlotek, but I was a little mad at them as well. Why didn't they pick mom up? Maybe she would have been healthy if she lived her life with them. Maybe Lars had been right, and her sickness was just a result of powers she didn't know how to use. Not that Lars knew about the shamanism. He thought mom was crazy. He thought I was going crazy as well.

With a grimace, I shook my head. No way was I going down that road. I hadn't believed mom was crazy before everything happened, so I wouldn't start believing it now. I was just glad Lars was out of my life.

"Ok," Jake said, parking the car.

Almost before the car stood still, the twins were off the roof and running toward the water. Elizabeth called after them before following. Magdalena cuddled closer to Eleanor, who wrapped her arms around the small child.

I looked through the window but couldn't see much, so I stepped out of the car.

We were parked on a field of brown, dead grass. The rain had turned to sleet as we went further North, and the wind seemed to have more bite to it than before. It pulled my hair this way and that, even as it was held in place under my hat. The ocean, not far away, was choppy and grey, the waves topped by white foam.

"Now where?" I asked Gudrun.

She couldn't understand me, but even before Jake had time to translate, she was walking.

Exchanging a glance, Jake and I followed.

Gudrun stopped at the edge of the beach, the water licking up around her naked legs and drenching the bottom of her borrowed dress.

The sound of the twins' laughter reached us, and I saw Magdalena look from where the sound came from and up at Eleanor. Eleanor noticed and looked at me.

"Go with her," I said with a smile as I wrapped my arms around myself against the cold. "Have fun. We'll be fine."

Narrowing her eyes but nodding, Eleanor squeezed Magdalena's hand and started leading her toward the other ghosts.

When I turned back, Jake was calling to Gudrun, trying to get her back on land. Standing as she did in the cold grey water, sleet falling around her, she looked otherworldly. It made me shiver.

Hearing her name, Gudrun turned and called back.

"There," Jake translated.

At his word, Gudrun nodded and pointed out over the water.

"What's there?" I called, not wanting to go into the water. I'd had enough of being cold for today, thank you.

Gudrun shook her head and stabbed her hand out over the water again.

With a sigh, I joined her, stepping into the waves. Water instantly soaked through my All-Stars, and the cold bit into my toes. I gasped, steeling myself not to run right back onto dry land.

When I stood by her side, Gudrun pointed again, and this time I squinted to see what she was pointing at. Through the sleet and the waves, I thought I saw an island. When I asked her if that was it, she nodded even if she couldn't understand me.

"Ok, how am I supposed to get over there?"

At this, she let her arm fall and shrugged. I wasn't sure if it was an answer to my question or because she couldn't understand. Either way, she stepped out of the water and headed back up to Jake.

With a sigh, I followed. When I reached her, Gudrun was talking in a low voice, almost drowned out by the sound of sleet against the ground and the waves on the beach. I was shivering, both from the cold in the air, and the cold of the water seeped into my shoes. I didn't want to be here. I wanted to go home and curl up in front of the fire, drinking Mrs. Hearth's hot chocolate with cinnamon, and watch a bad movie. I didn't want to stand in sleet with water-sogged jeans.

I was about to say all of this when Jake nodded and turned to me. "Gudrun says that from here, it's up to you. The other shaman is out on that island, and only you can reach him."

"How?" I asked through chattering teeth. This was getting ridiculous.

Jake shrugged. "By using your own powers, she said. Something about spirit recognizing spirit."

I glared at Gudrun. "I have no idea what that means."

She shrugged again, and I wanted to reach out and throttle her! Why couldn't she just tell me what to do? No, instead, she had to be all cryptic and say that spirit would recognize spirit. What did that even mean? Probably that I would know the shaman when I saw them, but how was I supposed to see them if they were on the other side of the water? How would I get there? Fly?

My shivering, my teeth chattering, even the world, seemed to stop for a moment, before it all rushed back and I grinned. "I can fly," I said, and Gudrun beamed back at me before she started to undress. "Hey, what're you doing?"

She only grinned and pulled off her dress. Before it hit the sodden ground, she was in the shape of a dove and flew into the air, circling above us.

Jake looked at me, smiling a lopsided grin. "You getting naked as well?"

I stuck my tongue out at him. "Nope. Or, a little. I'm getting out of my wet jeans and socks, and then I'm going to hide in the car until this is all over."

"Until what is all over?"

"I'm going to send my owl to look for the shaman."

"How does that work?"

"I have no idea, but I guess I'll learn on the fly."

"Hah!" When I just looked at him, his ears turned red. "Turn into a bird, learn on the fly?"

I snorted, and Jake grinned.

Picking up the discarded clothes, he followed me back to the car. We dumped the wet clothes in the trunk, and I slunk out of my clingy shoes, socks, and jeans, handing them to Jake to add to the trunk. For half a second I was thinking about being embarrassed for undressing in front of him, but it wasn't like he hadn't seen my naked legs before, so I decided against it.

As I got comfortable, I also thought about the fact that I would leave my half-naked body in the car with a guy I had barely known for two days, but there was no fear at the thought. I knew Jake wouldn't touch me, wouldn't even consider it. He wasn't that type of guy.

Sitting in the passenger seat with my legs tucked under me for warmth and my jacket thrown over my lap, I closed my eyes and reached within.

19

My owl had hardly moved since the fight with the wendigo. She had been badly hurt, and for a moment, I had been sure we would both die. Thankfully, we didn't, and when we merged back into one being, many of our hurts were mended. But we were still hurt; our ribs were cracked and our muscles sore. I could feel the area where bruises moved across my owl's wings, and I feared she wouldn't be able to fly.

When she felt my touch now, she stirred awake. I could almost feel her eyes on me, wondering what I wanted. The moment I thought it, the answer came, and I knew the owl knew what I knew. That was how we worked. Together.

While I knew what I wanted from the owl, the owl knew how to get it. As before, she moved out of my chest as soon as I permitted it, leaving a hollow where she used to sit. If the owl stayed out too long, the cold spot just under my breastbone where the ghosts were attached would start filling the area where she lived. I had no idea what would happen if it was completely filled with said cold, and I didn't want to find out.

It occurred to me then that I could probably just send the ghosts to look for the one person out on that island that could see them, but I also guessed it wouldn't be that easy. Gudrun had led me here, not my ghosts.

The owl turned her head to the side and looked at me. I knew she wished to fly, despite the weather.

The door still open, I picked up the owl and held my arms out of the car. With a last glance my way, the owl spread her wings. I could feel the ache in the wing joint for half a second before they flapped and she flew out of my arms, sleet hitting her face and gliding off the feathers without leaving a mark. The soreness in the joint was forgotten as soon as she got to a good height.

I was about to close the door and let the owl fly to find whatever spirit she was supposed to recognize, when a white dove landed on my arm. I jumped into the car, screaming in shock before realizing it was Gudrun.

She dug her claws into my arm until it felt like she would pierce both the fabric of my sweater and the skin. I glared at her, but her head was turned away the whole time, her beak pointing toward my owl.

"Fine," I growled. "I get it. You can stop hurting me now."

Pecking her beak against my clenched fist, she let go and flew away.

"What do you get?" Jake asked as he climbed into the driver's seat.

"That I need to be up there with the owl instead of down here," I said as I closed the door.

"How are you going to do that?"

"I have no idea."

He mumbled a ''good luck'' as I let the back of my seat fall into a lying position and curled up, trying to pull the jacket to cover as much of me as possible before I closed my eyes.

Ok, time to join with the owl without pulling her back into my body. How hard could it be?

I lay for a long time, listening to the sleet hitting the car and the wind making it rock on its wheels. Listening to Jake breathing and reading a book, and his phone ''wahoing'' regularly. Listening to my own breathing. It was when I heard my own heartbeat after close to fifteen minutes that I knew I was onto something.

Letting my muscles relax, I focused on my heartbeat. It was slow and steady, vibrating through my entire body, filling my veins with blood and oxygen. It was hypnotic, and soon I started falling. Or, that was wrong. It felt like I was falling, but when I opened my eyes, I hung in the air, one eye was looking at the grey world, the other looking at light blue fabric inside the car.

My breast tightened and it was hard to breathe. I felt my heart speed up and tasted panic at the back of my tongue.

Something white came through the sleet. My owl.

On instinct, I reached for her with both arms, and she gripped one of my hands with her claws and tugged. I flew out of the car and into the sky, unable to stop myself. Then my owl was there again, wings spread wide and aiming at my chest. I grabbed her, hugging the soft body to me, and we melted together.

Instead of her entering me, it was the other way around; I entered her chest. It was a weird feeling, as if I was entering a hot bath but at the same time like I was standing in a fast-flowing stream. Then I was standing still, or lying still. I wasn't sure. It was like I was sitting and lying and standing at the same time. I could feel my wings move to keep me flying even as I could feel my arms wrapped around my legs. My eyes were open and looking at the world around me, grey and cold but still very much alive, and at the same time I was looking at darkness. It was a warm darkness; pleasant and calm, and it was filled with the steady beat of a heart.

I let my arms and body rest and focused on flying.

It came naturally. Like I'd done it before, no need to learn. Which was good, because I really didn't want to take flying lessons in this weather and over the ocean.

Out of the grey came a white dove, Gudrun. She flew around me a few times, her small eyes blinking at me before she headed out across the water.

I followed out over the frothy ocean.

I would have loved the flight if it hadn't been for the weather. As we flew, I remembered the night before, and the freedom that had come with my owl-body. How I had wished to just disappear into the woods and live my life that way. But I hadn't. Instead, I was here, trying to fix all of this.

Narrowing my eyes and pushing my head a little farther down between my shoulders, I flapped on, trying to keep up with Gudrun.

Soon, brown land spread below.

We flew down and landed on a bench—Gudrun on the back and me on the seat. The body of a bird might be known to me, but I wasn't taking any chances on landing wrong, still hurting after the fight as I/we were. If the owl got hurt out here, there was no telling how we would get back together to heal each other.

And thinking while I was the owl and myself, and the owl was itself and me, was really weird.

The sleet thundering down around us, the ocean still wild, we waited.

Every now and again, the wind would bring with it the sound of someone crying. When I heard it, it felt like a wet mist slipped over my skin/feathers, and I knew without knowing that this was just the memory of sorrow, not something happening now.

It didn't help with the creep factor, however, so I moved a little closer to Gudrun for support.

The world was almost completely dark by the time someone came walking toward us. I blinked, glad for eyes that saw so well in the gloom.

At first, it looked like a man, then it wasn't a man at all, but a white moose. Then it was a man again, then a moose.

I blinked, trying to clean sleet from my eyes with hands I didn't have.

The man/moose stopped. He must have seen my clumsy movement. After half a heartbeat, he was walking again, straight for the bench this time. The closer he got, the easier it was to see, and I looked him over. When he was a man, he was under an umbrella, but when he was a moose, he seemed to repel the sleet and wetness like it wasn't there. I wish I knew how to do that. My feathers were soaked through by now.

The man/moose stopped in front of us, looking between Gudrun and myself.

"And who are you, pray tell?" He asked, his voice warm and curious.

For half a second I wasn't sure I would be able to answer, but then I did. It wasn't with my mouth/beak. It was more with my mind but still with my vocal cords, even if it didn't make any sense.

"I'm Lizzie, and I need your help."

It felt weird saying my name. It brought up a lot of bad memories, and I still wasn't sure I would keep it, but lacking anything else to call myself, it would have to do for now.

The man/moose blinked like he hadn't really expected an answer before he narrowed his eyes, and it felt like he was looking through me. Through the wet feathers and the skin underneath, to my small body/spirit/mind lying curled in a ball within, like a fetus in its mother's womb.

He pulled back, his brow knit, and turned to Gudrun. His eyes grew wide in surprise. I was pretty sure he didn't see the same in her as he saw in me, and I wondered what he'd seen at all.

"You are not of the People," he finally said, taking a step back from us.

"What do you mean?" I asked.

"She is not of the People," he pointed at Gudrun, then he moved his hand to point at me. "And I am forbidden to talk to those of your blood."

20

He was walking away before I even had time to consider what he was saying.

"Hey!" I flew after him, my wings twice as heavy with the soggy feathers, which made my muscles ache. Just thinking about trying to cross the water like this made me tired, but I had more important things to ponder. "What do you mean, you can't talk to those of my blood?"

The man/moose glanced over his shoulder and saw me flying after, if a little lopsided, and started walking faster. He was down at the shore and in a boat in seconds, but he didn't get it running before I was there as well.

I landed clumsily on one of the seats and glared at him as best I could.

"Now, listen here, dude. My life has been really weird lately, and I need answers! Like, really. I don't care if you're not supposed to speak with me or not, but I'm going to ride this boat to land with you, and I want you to answer my questions until we get there."

His hands hung limply by his side when he was a man, but when he was a moose, his head hung so low it almost touched the floor of the boat.

"Why can't you talk to me?" I asked as Gudrun landed beside

me, a lot more gracefully. "I promise I won't tell anyone, but I need answers, and you're the closest one that can give them to me."

He slumped down on the wet seat and buried his face in his hands. When he turned to moose again, he was just standing there, looking as sad as ever.

Finally, both his forms lifted their heads and glared at me. "Your blood has been banished," he said, pointing at me like his finger was a knife, and it would make me leave him alone. "I recognize that blood, and your family is not allowed to set foot on our holy lands ever again."

"Good thing I didn't then," I said, lifting one of my claws to indicate it wasn't really a foot at all. It only made his scowl deepen, so I pushed on. "Why isn't my blood allowed?"

He turned and started to work on the engine again. "Is that what you want to know? You only have the trip over before I shun you."

Stepping from one claw to the other, I thought fast, and then I let the story pour out of me. I told him about mom and how she died, and about how my death woke my shamanic powers and gave me necromantic powers as well. Then I told him about the ghosts and the wendigo. By the time my story was done, he'd stopped working on the engine and sat down again, listening intently.

"So, you see why I need help?" I asked. I was starting to feel both cold and tired, the hurts of my owl's body stronger now that the cold had had time to set in and the novelty of flying was gone. I just wanted to be alone with a hot bath right now.

"Yes," the man/moose answered, and that answer was just what I needed to hear. If owls could weep, I'm pretty sure I would have out of sheer relief that he hadn't sent me away.

"But I can't teach you how to do what you need to do."

I fluffed up my feathers in annoyance. "Why not?"

"Because how a shaman helps the ghosts of the world, the energy of the world, is individual. The People have their rituals, and I follow them, but I will not teach them to you."

"Because of my blood?"

"Yes. What I will do is tell you what we shamans are and how we help spirits and ghosts. That way, you can make your own rituals."

"I guess that's more than I can expect, my blood being bad and all."

He looked at me for a long moment, tugging at his fingers all the while, before he shook his head and returned to the engine.

It sputtered to life.

As his human form sat down, he patted the seat beside him. It took me a moment to realize he wanted me to join him. Clumsily, I flapped my way over there and breathed a sigh of relief when I didn't fly right over the end of the boat and into the water. I did not relish the thought of becoming an owl-sickle.

"Shamans have one job," the man/moose began as he steered the boat backward to get away from shore. "To heal. We feel the life of this world and the next, and do what we can to keep them in harmony."

"That's all well and good, but how do we do it?" I asked/thought.

"By making sure humanity doesn't take too much energy. That is a hard job in this day and age, but we try."

"How?"

"Let me explain. Everything around us is made out of one life-energy. The life of the Great One. Everything alive borrows from that energy until it cannot anymore. To borrow this energy, we need a link to the Great One, a root. This root runs from us and directly into that life-force. As we grow older, the root withers with us, or we wither because the root gets old, this no-one knows. Sometimes sickness makes the root wither faster, and sometimes a medicine can heal it. We shamans guide those whose roots are dying to their next stop. We show them the way to the Great One, so they do not stay behind and take more energy."

"But how do you know which root is withering and which is not?"

"We can see the roots."

"I can't."

"You haven't looked. Look, and you will see it reaching for the energy, the life force, of the earth."

I clicked my beak as I considered his words. "Ok, but what do you mean with people staying behind and taking more energy? Are those ghosts?"

"Ghosts, spirits of the dead, are the memories and what energy is left of them. Sometimes, if taken out of their life before their root has withered naturally, they will stay behind, frozen in place as they died. Their root will stay as well, and they will feed off the world when they do not need it anymore."

"But if they're just the memories and the energies of the people that die, don't that mean they really die when the root disappears? That if we sever that root, we kill them?"

"No, for they become part of the Great One. Their energy moves on to other living things. This is all part of life; nothing and no one ever really dies. They always live on in the world around us."

"I don't understand any of this."

"You do not need to, but you do need to heal the world. That is your job, despite what other powers you might have. A shaman heals."

"So, it is healing to kill ghosts?"

He stopped the boat. We were still out on the water, somewhere between the island and the beach. I could see them both through the sleet if I tried, but I was focused on staying on my feet/claws as the waves buffered the boat back and forth.

The man/moose turned to me, looking me hard in the eyes. "We do not kill ghosts. They move on to what is next for them and live on in us and everything else in the world. We return the energy to the Great One so she or he can live on and give life again and again."

"But is that all shamans do? Ki... move ghosts to the next part of their journey?"

His hard eyes softened. "We do that, and we try to heal the rest of the world. We can feel the roots of everything if we try, and that way, we may heal everything."

"I can heal rocks?"

He laughed. "Yes, if rocks need healing, but they will not accept it."

"What?"

He grabbed the motor stick again and steered us back on course. We'd drifted around and far away from the beach in the few seconds he hadn't pointed us in the right direction.

"Rocks are stubborn. They live for a long time and see many things. They know how the world works, so they will not accept healing if you offer it. Plants are not so stubborn and will take it. Some just live for a few months and want to savor it all. Others live for a long time but still want to live. We do what we can for them all."

"So we heal the world," I said slowly, looking but not really seeing Gudrun at the front of the boat. She'd turned into her human form again and was sitting, naked, with her arms spread and the sea and sleet spraying all over her. If she got a cold from this, I was not taking the blame. "We see the roots and try to heal the roots of those that need and want it, and let those that don't want it go. How do we know when we shouldn't heal?"

"You will know. That, we always know."

"How?"

"You will know."

"Ok. So can we heal anything other than the roots?"

"Sometimes. If someone is sick because their spirit is wrong, we have rituals to help right the spirit, but other than that, we need medicine like other humans."

"What do the root heal, then?"

"Everything, if it is meant to. Both the mind and the body."

"And how do I heal the root?"

"Depends on what kind of sick it is. A parasite needs removing, and some sickness needs cutting away, while others just need tending."

"But how do I know how to do either of those things?"

He glanced at me again, thankfully not letting the steering stick go this time. We were close to shore now, but I couldn't shake the feeling he wanted the conversation to go on. "That I am not allowed to teach you."

I snapped my beak a few times and fluffed up in annoyance. He grinned at me. Seeing a moose grin was a weird experience. This day had been nothing but weird experiences.

"The most important thing for you to remember," he continued. "Is to recharge. Our work take a lot of energy, both physical and mental, and I have known shamans who burn themselves out completely trying to help others."

"How do I recharge?"

He shrugged. "However you usually do after a long day of work, or arguing with a friend, or being sick. Take care of your body and mind. Eat more. You look thin. And learn how to do things the easy way."

"Like what?"

He booped my beak, and I wobbled on my feet, fighting to keep my balance. "Like spirit-walking. Your spirit animal is a guide, a friend, and you should not share her body unless you have to. You can leave your body just as you are."

"How?" We were almost at the shore now, and he was steadily minimizing his speed to give me more time.

"The same way you did now, but without the owl. It takes practice." He gave a rueful half-smile. "There are plenty of tutorials online about astral projecting and things like that. They are as good a teacher as any. It is a journey to find what works for you, however, so do not be discouraged if you can't do it right away."

He steered the boat onto shore and killed the engine before he stood and jumped into the water in one practiced movement. I noticed how he made sure to look everywhere else than right at Gudrun, who now was leaning over the edge of the boat to look at the water turn to sand as he pulled the boat out and up.

When the boat was secure enough not to slip out, he walked back into the water and flipped the engine so the rotors stood in the air, dripping saltwater, before he pulled the boat all the way up over the wave line.

"Come," he said and walked around the boat again. "I will carry you to your body. It is over there, yes?" He nodded in the direction of the car, even if we couldn't see it through the sleet.

I nodded, which must have looked weird with my owl head,

and waddled my way over the slippery seat. In front, Gudrun had jumped out of the boat and was running toward the car. Hopefully to get dressed.

The man/moose picked me up and turned, and almost dropped me as Eleanor appeared right in front of his face.

"What are you doing to her!" she yelled, trying to grab me out of the man/moose's arms.

He stumbled back, saying something in a language I couldn't understand, as I yelled: "Eleanor, it's fine! He's helping me."

The ghost stopped and blinked down at me. I wondered if she even knew it was really me inside this form or if she thought the man/moose had somehow kidnapped my owl. Either way, I was grateful to her.

"Ms. Lizzie?" asked Jonathan, leaning around Eleanor to look at me.

"Yes," I said/thought, surprised that they could hear me but at the same time not. "It's really me. He's just helping me. He's the one I came here for." Eleanor leaned back, carefully putting a hand over her big belly, and looked away, biting at the inside of her cheek. She was embarrassed, and I thought it might be the first time I'd ever seen that emotion in her. "Why don't you go to the car and I'll be right along? Ok?"

Before she could answer, the twins sidled past her to poke at me. I was so cold and soaked that I didn't expect to feel their fingers pass through me, so it was an even bigger surprise when they actually touched me. I was so startled that I pecked at their little fingers out of instinct before I'd even had time to consider what it meant that they could touch me.

The man/moose laughed at the startled sound I made, and the twins jumped back and stared at their fingers like they were magic.

"You're in spirit form now," he said. "They can touch you like this."

"But if I'm in spirit form, how can you touch me?"

"Because you are also part of the physical world. There are many details I do not have the time to teach you, so do not try to understand it. The power wants to be used, and you have the instincts. You will figure it out."

I grumbled, but before the twins could ask the man/moose any questions, Eleanor grabbed their hands and muttered something in French that I couldn't hear. She dragged them toward the car, Elizabeth following with Magdalena on her back. Magdalena kept glancing back at us, as if afraid for me, but she didn't say anything. Instead, she buried her face in Elizabeth's hair and made herself as small as possible.

"So those were the ghosts you told me about," the man/-moose said. It wasn't a question, but I answered in the affirmative anyway. I could feel his heart beat three times before he started walking after the ghosts, talking in a low voice all the while. "Do not interrupt me when I tell you this, you need to know, and we don't have much time. Your blood was banished from our lands generations ago. A shaman child died but came back, and he then knew how to control spirits in a way the rest of us did not. He got what you are now calling the necromantic powers, but we called it Spirit Brother or Sister. In itself, the power isn't bad, and there are other shamans through history who hold the same power. They were able to save spirits that didn't know they needed saving and to save humans from the spirits that go bad. They were great healers in our history. But this child, your ancestor, used his new powers for evil. He used the ghosts to spy on people for him and then used the information against others. The stories say we tried to teach him otherwise, that we gave him many chances, but when he used the powers to kill the girl he liked because she rejected him, he was banished. We severed his root and sent him away."

"Wouldn't that kill him?" I asked/thought, forgetting not to interrupt.

The car was within sight now.

"Yes, but it would also sever his power. He should not have been able to impact the spirits anymore. He never returned, and we thought him dead. Instead, he must have found someone and made his blood live on."

"When was this?" I asked, a bad taste filling my mouth and my stomach coiling in on itself. Could owls throw up?

"Close to fifty years ago."

I couldn't help the nervous flutter of my wings. "Then he's my grandfather."

"You know him?"

"No. My mother was abandoned at a church when she was only days old. She never knew her parents, and I never knew my grandparents."

He stopped beside the car.

"I am sorry for the grief this blood has caused you. When cutting someone's root, we don't destroy the power, and he must have given it to you."

The man/moose opened the door and set my owl on the chest of my sleeping human body. Immediately, I felt a tug at the back of my stomach, like something trying to drag me down into my body, but I fought it.

"My mother also had the powers," I said. "In some way."

He nodded. "I am not surprised. He was a strong shaman. I do hope what I have told you can be of some use. If you need me, let me know, but do not come here again. If anyone else of the People sees you on sacred land, they might return the favor of your grandfather."

"How can I contact you if I am not allowed here?"

"Spirit-walk," he said, a glint in his eyes. "Or use the internet. We are online, you know."

"Thanks," I growled, or tried to growl as much as an owl can, which wasn't much.

The man/moose smiled, and it was the first real smile he'd given me. As he moved to close the door, I remembered the other question I needed answers to.

"Wait!" He stopped but didn't turn back to look at me. "I mentioned the wendigo. How do I... it oppressed Connor, my father, how do I get him... un-oppressed?"

The man/moose's shoulders fell a little, and his hand tightened on the doorframe. When he spoke, his voice was so low I wasn't sure my human ears would have picked it up. "The only way to completely remove a wendigo is to kill the host. That will send the wendigo back to its original state. There are ways to bind the spirit within the host, but the only way to make sure it is gone, is by burning it." He turned and looked at me through the corner of one eye. "At least for us normal shamans."

He closed the door and disappeared into the sleet.

21

Grey fog. Light grey fog everywhere. Slipping into my nose and mouth. Spilling between my fingers like sand. I knew it and at the same time didn't. It was pooling between my breasts like water, wrapping itself around my arms and legs and middle, braiding itself into my hair. It filled my chest 'till it felt like my lungs would burst with it, spilling over my lips and dripping down my chin.

A "waho" broke through the dream, waking me.

"What is that?" I asked, starting to stretch.

"It's Klonoa," Jake answered.

A pang of pain jolted through my ribs as I moved, and I stopped. "What's a Klonoa?"

"It's a creature from this game –"

"Gotcha," I answered before he could start ranting.

I didn't know him well enough to know if he would actually rant, but both Sara and Mark had been into some form of geekery, and they always ranted about the things they loved. The joy in Jake's voice at the word was kind of cute, but I wasn't in the mood right now. Everything hurt.

"How long was I gone?" I asked.

"Just over an hour. It's late, but I've let Sara know we won't be back for a while yet."

"That's her you're texting with?"

"Yes."

"How did the dinner go?"

He sighed. "I think I'll let Sara explain that when we get home." He glanced my way. "If you got everything you need, I suggest we start the drive home right away. It will be a long one, and you look like crap." I managed a mock scowl, and he chuckled. "At least we've got soft, warm beds waiting for us."

"No," I said. "We need to fix this tonight. If things go well with the girl at the gas station, I fix Connor tonight."

Jake looked completely dumbfounded for a moment before his eyes lit with recognition. "I'm not sure it's such a good idea to do so much in one day. You're new to your power and you've already used it a lot today."

I smiled confidently. Or, I tried to smile confidently. "I'll be fine. I have an hour to rest before we reach the gas station, and then a few more hours before we get home."

"And what if things don't work out?"

"Then I'll have to think of something new."

"Do you have any idea how to do what you need to do?"

"Yes."

Now that I had the answer in my hand, I had to do something with it; I couldn't just wait when I could fix everything. Or at least something. A man had died because of the wendigo, not to mention all the spirits it had consumed.

Jake smiled. "I hope you'll let me question you when all this is over. There's so much for me to learn."

I couldn't help but laugh at that. "Sara said you were a geek, but not how much of one."

"I'll take that as a compliment."

He turned to Gudrun and spoke in a low voice.

I lay back onto the still laid-back seat and filled my ghosts in.

After a while, I noticed that both Jake and Gudrun were looking at me. "What?"

"Nothing," Jake answered before saying a few words to Gudrun and starting the car. "But Lizzie?"

It was strange. Hearing my name didn't bring on the same flood of sadness as before. It still brought some fear, but not sadness. Clicking my seatbelt in, I looked up at him.

"If you ever need to talk about what you're going through, I'm here. And I'm not just saying that because I want to know about your powers. I'm saying that because I like you, and Sara likes you, and I want to help."

I stared at him for a moment, guilt moving in my already queasy stomach. I'd kissed his girlfriend, and here he was, caring about me. It almost made me want to cry. Finally, I just smiled and thanked him. He nodded and started backing up the car.

Before I lay down, I reached for my phone. A green light was blinking in the upper right corner, letting me know someone had either called or sent a message. I worried it might be the police calling again, asking why I hadn't called them back or come running as soon as I heard the message, but it was only a text waiting for me. From Mark.

I glanced at Jake, feeling that guilt and shame move inside me again, before I turned away from him and opened the message.

It didn't say much. Mark wished me a good night and hoped the day had been a good one – or as good as I could have, everything considered. He then went on to let me know he would be going back to Toronto with the first train tomorrow. His phone was on and fully charged if I wanted to talk.

I stared at the message for a long time, not sure what to do.

Should I answer? If so, with what? A thank you? A simple ok? It felt like I should say more, but I wasn't sure what. What did him going back to Toronto tomorrow mean? Did he accept that I wanted to end us? Or was he going home to wait for me to come running back? For while it was clear to me that I had moved on, he had no idea what was going on. When I tried to tell Mark about the ghosts and shamanic powers, he called me crazy, and I knew he still felt that. What would he think if I tried to tell him everything else I'd been doing? Maybe he'd just ship me off to an asylum. Did boyfriends – or ex-boyfriends – have that kind of power in today's world? I didn't know, but it was a depressing thought.

Sighing, I turned off the screen and put the phone back in the mid-console.

"Anything important?" Jake asked.

I glanced at him, but his eyes were on the road, squinting a little to see through the dark and sleet.

"No. Just Mark saying good-night."

Jake nodded. "Anything you want to talk about?"

I opened and closed my mouth a few times, trying to figure out what to say. I wanted to talk about it, I realized, but with Jake? What would he say? Would he understand? And did that mean I had to tell him about kissing Sara? I could still feel her lips against mine, warm and comforting. And if I told him that, I would have to tell him what I felt about her, what I'd always felt about her, and what I wanted.

Jake met my eyes for a second before turning back to the road. He opened his mouth and closed it again as well, swallowing hard when he did.

I snorted. "We're like two beached fishes."

He chuckled. "Guess there's nothing to talk about then. Go

to sleep. You need to rest before we reach the station."

I didn't immediately lie down. I kept watching him, and I know he felt my eyes on him, for he fidgeted a little in his seat, changing his grip on the wheel a few times. It felt like there was something to talk about, something hanging between us, but I didn't know how to start that conversation. Instead, I turned my back to him again and closed my eyes.

22

We left the world we had known all our lives and entered this new one. This one we'd heard about from our Elders, whom had once lived here. It was said someone would open a door for us to return, to keep the world alive, but we did not believe it. A few of us had escaped through cracks in the Veil over the generations, never to return. Maybe they were why the world was still alive? Maybe they were dead and giving life to something else?

For we could sense so many dead things in this world. Things that had never been alive, but also things that had been alive but were now kept in death, unable to move on.

"Lizzie, wake up. We're here."

Jake's voice drew me out of what I'd thought would be an exhausted coma but turned into yet another dream. The content was already slipping away. Something about walking trees?

''Here'' was the gas-station we'd stopped at earlier. I'd been a little worried about getting to it, as it was on the other side of the freeway, but apparently there were ways, for Jake had parked us in the same spot as earlier.

I waited in the car while Jake got my jeans from the trunk. They were still damp, but I didn't care and managed to pull them on after some wiggling and cursing in the front seat. If

136

someone were to walk by, they would get an eyeful of my red underpants. At least I hadn't worn a thong today.

When dressed, I stepped out of the car and into the cold rain, and made my way to the main building. I didn't really want to go inside and risk meeting the guys or the kid again, even if it had been hours since we passed through last time.

I didn't have to enter, thankfully, as the woman I was looking for was standing right where she had earlier, looking in on the scene.

I stopped beside her and looked through the windows.

"Hello again," I said, and she jumped. Her eyes were huge with fear and expectation. I just hoped I could help her. "Remember me?"

She nodded. "You're the one that can see me." Her huge eyes narrowed. "You left."

"Yes, and I'm really sorry about that. I didn't know how to help you when I was here earlier, but I think I do now."

"So help me! I can't be here anymore, looking at this again and again and not able to do anything about it!"

She started crying.

"It will ok," I said. "But I can't do this here. Come on." When I started walking, the ghost followed. "What's your name?"

"Nina Eliot," she answered.

"Ok, Nina, I'm going to try something. I'm not really sure if it will work right away, but if I do it right, you should be able to move on, ok?"

"How will you know?"

"I just will."

She opened her mouth to say something but closed it again. Maybe she thought this hope was better than any other she'd had lately. That thought made me even sadder for her. How had her life, or afterlife, been? Being stuck looking at her own murder again and again. What does that do to a mind?

I stopped and looked around, then walked into the rain and climbed onto one of the tables standing on the brown lawn beside the gas-station.

"What're you doing?" Nina asked, following me into the open. The raindrops fell right through her.

"Getting in the zone," I answered as I twisted my legs until I sat in the lotus position. It would have been a lot easier without clingy, wet jeans, but I managed. "Stand there." I pointed to a spot right in front of me. She did as I asked. "Ok, let's do this."

Closing my eyes, I took a couple of deep breaths.

I felt the rain hitting me. Felt each drop as tiny individuals before they splattered across my soaked hair and joined with the others. I heard the drops hitting the ground around me. Heard my own heartbeat; hard and steady. Felt it through my entire being.

Eyes still closed, I reached out. It was the same I'd done when I let all the ghosts go last night, but this time I didn't grab anyone or anything; I just felt the world. And I felt so much.

I felt the energy running through the grass and the ground around me. The energy in every raindrop, like tiny spots of light in the dark that was the inside of my eyelids. I felt the energy running through the trees in the forest behind me. Even the energy in the asphalt on the freeway. The asphalt was dead, I realized, human made, but there were other things around it, under it, that lived and breathed and were fighting their way through the dead layer of stone. And there was life atop the asphalt. The energy of so many travelers going back and forth. It had created its own life. I felt the people inside the gas-stations on both sides of the road, and the people in the cars zooming by. I saw their emotions in a way I couldn't describe even to myself without getting lost in them for hours, maybe lifetimes. And there was Nina.

Her energy was much like the energy of the living, but it wasn't moving like the energy of everything else. It was dead, but also alive.

Opening my eyes, I held onto the image I'd had of the world, so full of light and life as it was, and saw it layered over everything in the real world. I still saw the light within the raindrops that fell, and the energy moving underground to everything living, sucked up through roots both real and not.

I could feel my own root connected to my spine and reaching down through the table I was sitting on and into the ground. It went deep and drank heavily of the energy, but it never took more than it was allowed.

And I could see Nina's root. It was shorter than mine, with few branches, but it was there. Like Nina's own energy, the root seemed frozen, somehow. Its colors were muted, like seen through a filter, and it didn't pulse with the life of everything else, even if it was drinking. It was more like the energy was flowed up it and into Nina on instinct, rather than being drawn there by life.

"Ok," I said, lifting my gaze and blinking in surprise.

Nina was the same as before, but at the same time not. She seemed hollowed out, like a shadow that wasn't quite there, fitting the idea of a ghost much better than how I usually saw them. There were lines of life running under her skin in thin streams that barely moved, collecting in her heart – that I could see through her chest as a glowing shape – and her eyes.

I cleared my throat. "I don't know if you're going to feel this or not, and I'm really sorry if it hurts, but it shouldn't."

She nodded and closed her eyes. All the muscles in her body tightened as well, like she was preparing herself for something she feared.

The way she did it made her even more alive in my eyes, and for a moment, I wasn't sure I could do this. If I did it right, she would stop being. She would be gone. But I also knew she didn't want to be here and I should respect that. Even knowing that, it didn't make the pit in my stomach any smaller.

Taking another deep breath, I focused on her root.

Again, I reached out, but this time I followed my vision, like I'd done when joining my owl. I stepped out of my own body, leaving it behind, and stepped into Nina.

I was pulled down through her and sucked back to her root before I had a chance to react. When reaching it, I grabbed the side of it, not letting it pull me into the earth. I feared I might be pulled into every single straw of grass if it happened and have no way of getting back into my own body.

Nina's root was as still from the inside as it had looked from the outside. How to sever it? I could feel my own heart beat in my body several times as I hung there, unsure what to do. Then I pulled myself against the root and merged with it as I'd merged with Nina.

The root was its own entity. Like my owl was me and not me at the same time, so was the root. It was tired, so tired. All it wanted was to rest.

I let my body/spirit flow out until I was in every part of the root, filling it with warmth and life it hadn't felt in so long. Then, in a second, I changed myself. I pulled myself tight, like a rubber band, and saw myself sharp as a blade.

I cut through the root where it was connected to Nina.

For a long heartbeat, we hung still. I was connected to both

Nina and the root, energy flowing through me into her. Then I let the root go.

Everything after that happened so fast.

I flew out of Nina the second I let go and crashed into my own body with such force that I lost my breath. Through teary eyes, I saw Nina open her mouth in what for one second looked like a scream, then turned to laughter.

As I looked on, she started to dissolve: her energy pulled apart by every raindrop that hit her, and it slipped into the soil she was standing on, or was pulled into the air until there was nothing left. At least nothing I could see with the naked eye.

When I reached out with my powers, I could still feel her energy around me, in the water the earth was drinking, or in the wind that caressed my face.

And I cried. Not the tears of the surprising lack of oxygen or pain, but tears of joy.

I stayed curled up on the table until the spirit-vision dulled into hardly anything. It still lay like a second shadow over everything, but not so much so that I became dizzy every time I tried focusing on anything else.

When I could move again, I stopped by the gas station to use the toilet to dry off a little. The teenager behind the counter looked at me with a furrowed brow, trying to recognize me, both when I came in and when I walked out again almost half an hour later, a little drier than before.

As I climbed into the car, Jake put away his phone.

"How did it go?" he asked, a furrow in his brow. Was he worried?

"Good, actually," I said as I clicked on my seatbelt. "Really good."

His frown turned to a smile. "That's good." He turned and said something in German, and Gudrun answered around a half-eaten sandwich. When Jake turned back, his eyes were tired but warm. "I gave the rest of your sandwich to Gudrun. She was hungry, and I didn't want to run into the station."

I smiled back. "No worries. I wasn't going to eat it anyway."

"That's what I thought." He held a granola bar my way. "But you should eat this."

I scowled but took the bar, crinkling the wrapper extra loudly as I opened it.

Jake started the car and pulled out of the parking lot. "So, I got another message from Sara while you were... doing your thing."

"Oh?" I said around a big piece of the granola bar. It was like dust in my mouth, seeming to grow with each bite. Jake must have noticed, for he handed me a bottle of sparkly water with raspberry-taste. I took a gulp to help swallow the food.

He took a deep breath before speaking: "Abigail didn't want to listen to her or Mrs. Hearth, and kept demanding for them to call you back so she could take you away. After a while, she left in a rage." I looked at him and took another bite of the bar. "But she didn't stay gone. When Abigail returned, she brought some of her cousins with her."

I almost spat out the piece. "What?"

"Calm down, Mrs. Hearth didn't let them inside, but they did make a fuss. Mrs. Hearth had to claim Hearth and Home for them to go away."

"Hearth and Home?"

Jake waved a hand as if it wasn't important. "It's a witch custom. A witch can give sanctuary to anyone they want, and other witches can't touch them as long as they stay inside their boundaries without breaking our laws. She's claimed Hearth and Home for you." He said it flippantly, trying to make it seem like a small thing, but I noticed how his hands were gripping the wheel a little too tight, and how his jaw was clenched.

I turned away and stared out the front window. The rain kept thundering down, the window-wipers barely keeping it at bay.

"They really want to burn me, then? That wasn't an exagger-ation?" My voice sounded hollow.

One of my ghosts said my name, but I didn't hear which one. All of them were worried, two of them on the edge of shock. Or I might have been on the edge of shock and mirroring my own feelings into them. I didn't know.

A hand landed on my knee, and I looked up to meet Jake's grey eyes for a second before he focused on the road.

"It will be ok, Lizzie. We've got you, ok? We won't let them touch you. Mrs. Hearth has informed the Council of the situation, and they have reinforced the Hearth and Home. If anyone takes you from Mrs. Hearth's land, the Council will know and will bring you back."

He squeezed my knee before returning his hand to the wheel again. A warm spot remained where his hand had rested, and I stared at it until it faded.

"Did anything else happen?" I asked, moving my eyes from my knee to my hands. I was chipping away at the flower-polish and stopped myself, but the damage was already done. And here I'd been so happy with it.

"No. Sara and Mrs. Hearth controlled the wards and set a couple of new ones, then stayed up a little longer to make sure nothing else happened. Mrs. Hearth had to go to bed first. These last few days have taken a lot out of her." A stab of guilt moved through my stomach. "And Sara followed. I don't think she could stand staying up alone after the day she's had."

I nodded. "Even if she knows her mother, she can still be disappointed by her." I knit my fists into each other so hard it hurt. "It's worse with family, really. We keep hoping they will change. That they will finally understand what they've done wrong, even when we know there's no use."

"Speaking from experience?"

I snorted. "Just recently. Things weren't so bad for me,

actually. My family accepted me for who I was, but then Connor left, and I kept expecting him to come back, to make things right. When he finally did... well, you know how that went."

We drove in silence for a minute.

I leaned my head back against the seat and closed my eyes, listening to the motor and the rain. My ghosts were whispering in the backseat, and Gudrun was humming to herself. It all sounded so normal, so carefree. Like nothing in the world was wrong, and all the emotions inside of me weren't real.

Jake cleared his throat, and I opened my eyes and turned my head to look at him.

"Have you thought about how to deal with Connor? I heard what the shaman said at the end..." The sentence trailed off into nothing, but I could still hear the words he didn't say. That the shaman told me the only way to deal with a wendigo was to kill the host. At least for a typical shaman.

I closed my eyes and turned my head away again. "I can't kill him," I said. "And I can't let anyone else do it either. But neither can I let him out. He has killed someone, eaten them, and that family deserves justice. Deserves to know what happened. But I can't turn him over to the police either. What will I tell them? That he suddenly went mad?"

"It is an excuse that has worked before," Jake murmured.

"I have to do something. This is my mess. I created the Rift in the Veil. I have to fix it again." A long, expectant silence filled the car. My ghosts had stopped talking, and even Gudrun had stopped humming. Like she understood we were discussing something important. "The shaman said ''for a normal shaman'', which means there might be something I can do. Gudrun said I could control every spirit that has passed through the Grey World, and the wendigo did that. So I'll try to force it out of Connor. To command it to leave its host and to die."

"You think that will work? Do you even know how to tell a command?"

"I've done it before, I can do it again."

"And do you think it will die from your command? That it won't fight you?"

"I'm sure it will."

"You need a plan B."

I opened my eyes and glared through the front window. "Any suggestions?"

He glanced at me and grinned. "Actually, yes."

24

Ever since Sara let it drop that Abigail was used to dealing with ghosts, I'd wondered how that worked. According to the witches, spirits weren't a regular part of our world - not before I ruined the Veil, anyway - so how could Abigail be used to dealing with ghosts and spirits? How could any witch? As Jake laid out his plan, he gave me the answer.

While spirits and monsters had been locked away in their own world when the Veil was created, there were places where the Veil was weak, and these monsters could slip through. It was then the job of the witches in the area to track and capture this creature, for so to return it to the Spirit World.

And there were the ghosts. Ghosts of humans that had died were a natural thing in our world, as my own fright had proven. Unlike the ghosts I'd dealt with so far, who had been kind if impatient and a little annoyed, some spirits were malicious: poltergeists and other forms of lost souls that wandered our world and did damage.

None of the magic-users had ever expressly taken on the task of dealing with these spirits, so they all did it in their own way. Witches trapped them, and that was what Jake was proposing now.

It could work. At least we thought so, until Jake told Gudrun

147

our plan. After a lot of back and forth, Jake sighed and turned to me again.

"According to Gudrun, we can't kill the wendigo," he said.

"What? Why?"

"Until the Veil is repaired, it will keep coming back."

"How?" My voice was too loud and I cleared my throat, trying again, lower this time. "How?"

"Spirits that aren't of our world can't die here. We have always thought we killed them with our rituals, but instead, we just sent them back to the Spirit World. Until now, it has worked well. It was hard for them to come back to our world. But now, with the Rift and the many other openings..." he let the sentence trail off.

"They will keep coming back," I said.

Jake nodded.

I chewed on my thumbnail for a few seconds. "Could Gudrun go back to the Spirit World? Kill it there?"

Jake asked, but it was clear by Gudrun's tone that she was not happy about that.

"No," Jake confirmed. "She will not kill a spirit that doesn't directly threaten her or the balance of the worlds. The wendigo does not do this. But when we return it to the Spirit World, it will have to travel to the Rift and then through the Grey World again, which will take time, and it will be back to its original state."

"The shaman said the same," I said in a low voice, not even sure I'd spoken aloud.

Jake nodded. "Right. So we banish it and when it returns, we know how to deal with it!"

"Why can't we keep it bound? Why do we have to banish it?"

"Because it can break loose from the binding. It's not a foolproof solution when it comes to these kinds of spirits. If it breaks loose... well, it can be really dangerous to the witch that did the binding."

"Ok. We're not putting Sara in danger to make things easier."

Jake nodded, and we descended into discussing how to deal with the wendigo whenever it came back.

"What about us?" The twins asked during a lull in the conversation. "We want to help."

I was already shaking my head. "Nope. You are all going to stay at my house, where you are partly safe. The wendigo couldn't get in there earlier, so it shouldn't be able to do so now either. Speaking of, why couldn't it get in?"

Jake shrugged. "I don't know. We can try to cast some spells and check for wards. I know Mrs. Hearth keeps some wards on your house, but the wendigo got into her house, so her wards weren't strong enough to keep it away."

"But why can't we help?!" Johana moaned.

"Because I will not be putting your lives in danger! How many times do we have to go through this?" I snapped.

The twins stared at me with big eyes, and Magdalena looked even more scared than usual. Elizabeth was already talking to her siblings, however, trying to tell them the same thing as me. I was glad I had her on my side. They listened to her, even if they teased her a lot.

"The ghosts?" Jake asked.

I nodded and told him.

It was still a long time before we reached Sky Harbour, so we stopped and I drove for a little bit, letting Jake take a powernap. He wouldn't let me drive all the way home, however, so he'd put on an alarm and slept for ninety minutes before he ordered me back in the passenger seat to relax. I was the one with the new powers wishing to over-use them, after all.

I didn't sleep, though, only stared out the window at the dark world around us until we finally left the highway, when I picked up my phone and called Sara.

It was almost one in the morning, and I knew both she and Mrs. Hearth had had a long day. So had Jake and me, but we'd both agreed to fix this problem before any new ones could crop up. To do that, we needed Sara's help. Mrs. Hearth needed to help out as well, but we didn't need her before we were finished.

Sara was not happy to be woken up, but when I told her what we needed, her lust for adventure kicked in, and she was wide awake. She was a little disappointed I didn't want her to do more right now than inform Mrs. Hearth of her role and prepare for our return, though.

While I didn't share her joy of going head-to-head with a wendigo, I did feel a kind of grim satisfaction. I was going to fix this problem right now, and that felt good.

Jake cleared his throat as soon as I put the phone down. "I just wanted to let you know, the car behind us was parked in the woods and slipped out after we drove past."

I glanced in my side mirror but couldn't see anything.

We were on the forest road running around Sky Harbour and into our neighborhood. The road was created for people living here but working in Halifax or Dartmouth, so they didn't have to drive through town to get home, but it didn't have any streetlights, and few used it at this hour.

"You won't see it yet," Jake said as if reading my thoughts. "Their front lights are off, but I think it might be one of the witches. They would recognize Mrs. Hearth's car."

"Do we need to worry?" I asked, turning to look at him.

"I don't think they'll run us off the road if that's what you're afraid of. As long as we don't have to stop before we reach Mrs. Hearth's land, it shouldn't be a problem."

I wanted to believe him, wanted to believe it wasn't a problem, but he was gripping the steering wheel in a way I'd come to recognize as nervous.

Turning, I looked into the backseat. Elizabeth was sleeping with her head against the window, Magdalena snoring with her head in her lap. So far, I'd never seen my ghosts sleep, I didn't think they needed it, but maybe they did it anyway? As a way to pass the time? Eleanor was staring past them and out the window, but she felt my eyes on her and met my gaze. Gudrun was sleeping on her other side. The twins were nowhere in sight, but I could feel them up on the roof, so I gave a small tug on the thread between us.

Instantly, they popped their heads through the ceiling.

"Would one of you mind checking out the car following us?" I asked. "It has its front lights turned off for us not to see it. Jake thinks it's the witches that want me."

Almost before the words were out of my mouth, both ghosts drifted backward and disappeared from the car. For a split second, I could see them standing in the middle of the road; a boy and a girl, dressed in matching blue outfits from the 1800s, both blond and cute as could be, holding hands. Then they were gone, swallowed by the darkness.

Shivering, I turned forward again. I'd seen *The Shining* once, and the twin girls there would forever be overpowered by Johana and Jonathan standing on that road now. It was an eerie image.

Elizabeth and Magdalena had woken up when I tugged on the threads, and they were still turned back as if waiting for the twins to reappear.

The road made a turn and houses and streetlights replaced

the dark forest landscape. The houses grew grander and older as we climbed a hill until we turned onto McKey-street. Here, every house was a Victorian of some kind, but none as big or grand as the three-and-a-half-story Queen Anne standing at the top of the street. Key-house. My childhood home. This whole street had once been our property, as well as the forest around it, but my family sold off a lot of it, and an old, grand neighborhood was the result.

At the top of the hill, in front of my house, the road came to an end in a round-about. Besides Key-house, the round-about led to two other homes; Mrs. Hearth's and the Norris's. We leased the land to them, as well as the two houses below them. The woods leading in all directions around the houses belonged to us as well.

As Jake drove around the round-about, I looked up at my home. The lights were still on after this morning, and it looked surprisingly warm and welcoming in the rainy night.

"And there they go," Jake murmured, making me turn to see what looked like a red VW Beetle with its front lights turned off drive into one of the driveways down the street.

Instantly, the twins' returned, standing outside my window like the props in a horror movie.

Taking off my seatbelt, I opened the door. "Well?" I didn't take my eyes off the car.

No-one had stepped out yet.

"There were two women in the car. They did not say anything, but they did curse when Mr. Jake stopped the car," Johana said.

"The one riding along ordered the other to park, to make it looked like they belonged, and the one driving turned into the driveway just down there," Jonathan finished, and both twins turned as one to point at the red car.

I told Jake what the twins had said. He hadn't even taken off his seatbelt, but now he grunted and did so.

"We should just get inside," he said as he stepped out into the rain.

I followed suit as he opened the door for Gudrun.

Walking toward the house, I thanked the twins. They beamed in joy, and I couldn't help smiling myself, before I said in a low voice: "Now, could I ask you two to keep an eye on that car for me? And the witches inside it?"

"Yes," Jonathan answered. As if they shared a mind, Johana continued: "But why?"

The rest of my ghosts were close behind me as I hurried up the porch steps and stopped under cover of the porch roof. In the driveway, Gudrun was dancing in a circle, her arms spread wide. Jake was shaking his head and jogged to catch up with me.

"I don't want any of you near the wendigo when we do what we now plan to do," I said. "I can't risk any of you getting hurt." The twins glanced at each other, and I turned to Eleanor, Elizabeth, and Magdalena. "I want you to wait at home, ok? Stay there until I ask you to come." I turned back to the twins. "And when the witches leave, you two are to join the others there, ok?"

"But we want to help," Magdalena said, a stubborn pout on her face.

The thread between us was vibrating with something I had never expected to feel from the girl. Shame. Shame that she was so scared, and that she hadn't fought more to help me earlier.

I knelt to be face-to-face with her. "The best way you can help me right now, is by staying safe, ok? The wendigo has already taken two of you away from me. I will not let it take anyone else."

Magdalena's pout changed from stubborn to scared, and she buried her face in the pink folds of Elizabeth's dress. I stood, daring the other ghosts to argue. They all turned to Eleanor, who gave a small nod before she reached out and took Magdalena's hand.

As if that was their cue, the twins disappeared from view. I felt their thread shift down the street but didn't turn to look at them. Instead, I watched the rest of my ghosts walk across the round-about and up the driveway, disappearing into the shadows of my home. Gudrun was with them. She had wanted to help out, but after a lot of back and forth, we agreed she would best serve as a guardian for the many ghosts hanging around me. Our plan heavily rested on my powers and the rituals of the witches, and having Gudrun with us might give the wendigo the extra will to fight back, and so she would guard the ghosts in case the wendigo got away from us. She could fight it if it tried to get to them.

"You ready?" Jake asked from beside me.

I sighed and turned toward the door. "As ready as I'll ever be." Jake opened the door, and as we stepped inside, I asked: "Why would my ghosts walk to the back instead of going through the front door?"

Jake glanced at me as he closed and locked the door. "You mean your house?" When I nodded, he continued: "Because of the fence. 'tis iron. Iron and salt repel ghosts."

"Oh," I said, not knowing what else to say.

"Took you long enough," Sara said as she stepped from the living room, a cup of coffee in her hands.

"My apologies," Jake said as he kissed Sara on the cheek. It didn't sound like he meant it, but Sara seemed happy enough.

It made me smile a little.

She grumbled but didn't say anything else as she handed the cup to her boyfriend. When he took it, Sara's eyes jumped from him to me and back again, and she cocked her head slightly.

Taking a sip of the coffee, Jake shook his head almost imperceptibly.

If I hadn't been watching them, I wouldn't have noticed, and I wouldn't have wondered what it meant. Now, I did wonder. It felt like they were hiding something, and I didn't like it. I had never liked it when Sara hid things from me, but knowing she did it with someone else now, hurt even more.

Instead of dwelling on the feeling, I put my shoes by the wall and walked past them, heading toward the attic. They could have their secrets. I had a wendigo to take care of.

25

As I walked away, I could hear Sara and Jake whispering.

"You didn't tell her?" Sara asked.

"No," Jake answered. "It felt wrong doing it without you."

"Awww, that's stupid." I heard a smack that sounded a lot like Sara hitting his arm. "What do you think she'll think 'bout having been in the car with you for half a day, and you not saying nothing?"

"It'll be fine, Sara. I'm sure Lizzie will respect our attempt at respecting her."

Whatever Sara answered, it was lost to me as I stepped onto the first-floor landing. I almost wished I hadn't sent all the ghosts over to my place. I was curious now, and having one of them spy on Sara and Jake would be perfect. Wouldn't be too respectful, though, and I couldn't keep remembering what the shaman had said about my grandfather and how he used his powers for his own gain. I sighed and started up the next set of stairs.

Hurried steps warned me just before Sara and Jake joined me, and we walked in silence until we reached the attic.

When I was here last – was that just this morning? – the altar held a chalice, a knife, candles, and some other stuff I couldn't even pretend to remember. Now, it held a candle, two pieces of string, and a split geode, the clear quartz interior glinting in the overhead light.

To the left of the altar lay Connor. He was still dressed in the clothes we'd caught him in; blood-soaked shirt and missing a shoe. Someone had tied a rope around his shoulders and chest, the end lying across the floor and almost to the wall. A perfect circle had been drawn in chalk around him, with signs I didn't recognize on the outside. Four white rocks stood on the circle-line, making a perfect box around his still body.

For some reason, I couldn't stop staring at his foot—the one missing the shoe. I remembered him telling me, again and again, to wear socks, for I always started sneezing if I didn't. Even in summer, I'd sneeze, and he'd tell me to wear socks.

Movement pulled me out of the memory, and I watched as Sara walked to the altar. Without a word, she lit the candle with a lighter from her pocket. I walked closer, watching as the fire caught. The candle was white with herbs showing just under the surface here and there.

After making sure the flame was steady, Sara put the two pieces of thread across each other. One of the threads was completely white, the other looked almost blond.

"Is that hair?" I asked, recognizing the blond color. It was Sara's natural color, bright and warm.

"Yeah," Sara answered, making sure the threads lay perfectly. "It makes the trapping-spell stronger."

I didn't answer, my eyes jumping back to Connor.

A bucket filled with ice-water stood to his left, well outside of the circle, and three smoked quartz clusters, stood parallel to the crystals in an unfinished square outside the circle.

As if knowing what I was looking for, Sara lifted a similar rock from her pocket and put it on the altar.

I stared at Connor for a long moment, memories flickering inside my head. Him as my dad, taking care of me, holding me while I cried, yelling at me for sneaking out, teaching me how to treat old books and antiquities. Memories of him leaving, of his return with Cornelia and Catherina, of him yelling at me as I watched my aunt die, of his black eyes when the wendigo oppressed him.

"What will happen when I force the wendigo out of him?" I asked, my voice a little too high.

"We don't know," Jake answered. "No-one in my line has ever managed to remove a oppressing spirit from their host. We do know that the spirit eats at the host's soul, but we don't know how long it takes before the soul is completely gone, or how the body will function without a soul or spirit controlling i... ouch!"

I turned to see Jake rubbing his upper arm and Sara glowering at him. When she saw me watching, her face softened and she walked across the floor to wrap her arms around me. She was almost a head shorter than me, but she enveloped me none the less.

"It'll be ok," she said.

I hugged her back for a brief second before forcing myself away. "The plan is clear?"

Sara stepped back and walked around the circle, eyes on Connor. "I break the sleeping-spell and remove the shock-crystals. He won't wake right away, so that's not a problem. The hard part comes when Jake wakes him."

Jake walked past me. "Which I do by throwing this bucket of water on him."

"I need to place the fourth cage-crystal instantly, so the wendigo can't escape," Sara continued.

"Then it's up to me," I walked to stand at Connor's feet, just outside the invisible line of the cage-crystals. "I force the wendigo out of Connor, and Jake pulls him out." Jake nodded when I looked at him.

"After that, it depends on how you're powers work," Sara said. "If you can't command the wendigo to die, I trap it like any other spirit, and we can burn it together."

I met her eyes and we nodded in unison.

"Ok," I said, taking a deep breath. "Let's do this."

26

It took me a little over a minute to turn on my spirit-vision, but when it clicked, it felt natural and easy. Like I should have had it on all the time.

I opened my eyes and looked around the room. There were traces of magic everywhere. It pulsed from the crystals and the candle, and oozed from the chests and the altar. Sara's luck was flaring around her in a bright golden dome, and I could see a dark blue shadow moving around Jake's head and down his neck. Was that his power?

Reluctantly, my eyes went to Connor; the black shadow of the wendigo-spirit clung to him like a second skin, and it pulsed outward, almost hiding the too small human body within the mass of the wendigo.

Removing the sleep-spell and the shock-crystals took seconds, then Sara picked up the smoky quartz cluster she'd placed on the altar earlier and walked to her spot, crouching and holding the cluster just over the floor. I'd worried that Connor wouldn't be able to exit either, but Sara had changed the spell on the crystals to only cage spirits, not humans, so that shouldn't be a problem.

Sara looked to Jake and nodded, and he turned toward me and mimicked her movement. Drawing another deep breath, I nodded back.

Lifting the bucket, Jake walked to stand just outside the cage and flung the water toward Connor.

I saw the water arch through the air as if in slow motion before the sound of stone touching wood vibrated through me, and the cage shimmered up around Connor.

I almost took a step back, the cage wall millimeters from my face, but I stayed where I was, eyes glued to Connor as the water splashed down and he gasped and spluttered for air.

The dark shadow that was the wendigo pushed up and surged toward me, dragging the human body after it. It looked unnatural; like Connor was just a rag doll controlled by a child.

Connor and the wendigo slammed into the wall just in front of my face. They didn't bounce back, like I'd expected. Instead, the wendigo smashed Connor's face against the wall and snarled at me, dragging his lips along the wall and leaving a line of bloody spit.

I wanted to look away, but couldn't. The blood coating his teeth was fresh. That was Connor's blood. Not his victim's. That couldn't be good.

I forced myself to look away from the bloody teeth and the completely black eyes, and focused on the wendigo's head, hovering just over Connor's.

The wendigo didn't have eyes. Its head was that of a wolf's skull with antlers, but no flesh or eyes or muscle. Still, I felt it when our eyes met. It was like an icy chill ran down my back and settled in my stomach. It made my owl flutter her wings in discomfort, and I felt the worry of my ghosts surge through the threads connecting us, answering my own uncertainty.

I wanted to call to them, wanted them to be here and stand beside me, but I wouldn't. I wouldn't put them in danger like that. Instead, I reached forward with my power, both shamanic and necromantic.

With my spirit-vision on, I could see the root running from Connor and into the ground. It was small, and falling apart even as I watched. Black lines that looked like fungus ran around it, breaking it open and forcing its way inside it. Taking it over.

The moment I saw those black lines, something inside me rose into my throat. It was the same power I'd used yesterday, when I bound all those ghosts to me. Whatever it was, it pushed against the inside of my skin, making me shiver with cold.

"Wendigo," my voice sounded far away, somehow.

"I command you," grey tendrils of mist and fog curled at the edge of my vision. Glancing down, I saw the mist spilling from my skin, and the chilly sensation suddenly made sense.

Inside the cage, the wendigo stepped back, dragging Connor along.

The fog reached through the wall between us and toward the wendigo.

"To leave your host."

The tendrils shot forward and grabbed the shadow of the wendigo. My magic crept up his legs and twined around his arms, his throat and his chest.

I felt a new thread in my chest. It was dark and cold, thin, and twitching to get away from me, but my owl grabbed it with both claws and held on. The thread now bound the wendigo to me.

"Leave your host," I repeated as my magic tightened around the shadow.

It trashed against my hold, screaming in a high pitched tone I was sure would wake every neighbor for miles around. It hurt my ears, but I didn't move to cover them. Instead, I focused the pain it created into the thread between us to strengthen my grip on him.

"I command you to leave your host!"

My voice rang in my ears, amplified by the magic spilling around and from me, reaching vines into the cage to wrap around the wendigo, slowly filling the magically sealed area with light grey fog.

Something clicked inside me and the thread between me and the wendigo stopped trying to get away. I couldn't help but smile. The cold sensation of mist caressed my lips. The wendigo was mine.

I lowered my eyes to Connor's root, and before I could even consider my actions, I was diving into it.

The fungus was everywhere, leeching off Connor's life force and energy. And I knew, just like the shaman had said I would, that this root was sick. In the same way, I knew what to do with it.

Even as the dark tendrils turned their attention to me, I turned mine on them. The mist pushing through my pores swirled closer to me for a second before I sent it out, reaching for each and every thread at once.

I could hear the wendigo snarling, no longer afraid but enraged. I could feel my hold on him strengthen, but my body weakening. I was tired.

Inside the root, my magic was eating away at the dark tendrils, consuming them, making them their own. I wasn't sure if it was the grey magic or another kind of magic anymore. The shamanic power to heal and the necromantic power to control seemed to merge.

Outside, my body fell to its knees, and I was pulled back into it. I gasped in exhausted pain, inhaling the mist around me, and reached out again. My magic was still forcing the tendrils away from the root, sealing the holes as it went.

Relieved, I lifted my gaze to the wendigo. "I command you to leave your host!" I called, and my voice shattered the last of the black fungus on Connor's root.

Looking up, I felt tears running from my eyes, but I blinked them away. The wendigo had gone silent, finally listening to my commands, and just stood there.

On the other side of the cage, Jake had pulled Connor out and was checking his pulse. By the altar, Sara stood with the split geode in her hands. Her eyes jumped between the cage and me. I didn't know if she could see the wendigo or not, but her eyes brimmed with worry and she was bouncing on her toes, as if she wanted to run to me.

I turned back to the wendigo, meeting its empty eye sockets. I felt my power soar through me. It felt like the after-waves of orgasm, my body just as tired as it might be then, but that good feeling slipping through my muscles and my blood. It felt like a high, like I could go forever even as I was having trouble focusing my eyes because I was so tired.

"Die," I said, sending the command through the many strands binding the wendigo to me.

The power slammed into something and was flung back. Right into me.

A splitting pain raced through my head, making my vision blur and the world spin around me.

"Sara," I said, my voice groggy, as if I was drunk. Instantly, she stopped moving. "I can't."

Her worried eyes took on a hard shine, and the gold I'd seen flickering there surged outward as she turned her eyes to the cage and lifted the geode, one piece in each hand, the crystals toward the cage.

I closed my eyes and turned off my spirit-vision as her voice rang out, echoing off the white walls and being thrown around the room. The thread between me and the wendigo held, and I felt it move toward the witch.

Hands touched my shoulders, and I looked up to see Jake by my side.

When I turned back to Sara, she was tying the strings around the geode, her eyes still glowing yellow, making her shine with magic. She looked otherworldly and powerful and beautiful.

The wendigo was still standing like it had when it repelled my command, still and empty, but it thinned into smoke as I watched, floating toward Sara and the geode.

Letting Jake help me into a sitting position, I leaned against him, and together, we watch as Sara continued mumbling her spell and dripping the wax of the candle along the crack in the geode, sealing it. One of the herbs caught fire and sent a plume of smell into the room. Rosemary.

The moment she finished her spell, Sara turned and ran to me, skidding to a halt on her knees in front of me and lifted my face, looking into my eyes.

"Lizzie?" her voice was shaking.

"I'm here," I mumbled, voice still weak and slurred. I felt drunk.

Sara let out a sigh and touched her forehead against my shoulder. Her back started shuddering, and it took me a second to realize she was laughing. It sounded a tad hysterical, and I couldn't help but laugh with her. From behind me, Jake started chuckling as well, the vibrations running through his chest and hurting my ribs, but I didn't care. I just laughed and laughed, letting them both embrace me.

27

Our laughter must have been the universal signal that our fight was over, for while Sara, Jake, and I still sat huddled on the floor, someone knocked at the door.

Before we could answer, it opened, and Mrs. Hearth walked in. She barely glanced at us before she hurried to Connor's side.

At the same time, I felt the threads in my chest twinge with worry, and I knew my fright of ghosts was considering coming over to see how things were going and figure out what the sudden relief meant. It was good to know they couldn't read my mind, but I still didn't want them here. The wendigo was just bound, and Jake had said it could break free. If it did, I did not want my ghosts to be the first thing it ran across.

"How is he?" Jake asked, bringing my focus back to the room and the situation at hand.

I hadn't given Connor much thought before, intent on the wendigo, but now I turned to look his way.

Connor lay on the floor; his head tilted, face turned my way and bloody foam was dripping from the corner of his mouth.

My fingers dug into Sara and Jake's flesh as I tried to continue breathing. Why wasn't he waking up? He should be waking up!

"Jake, come over here and help me," Mrs. Hearth said, not taking her eyes of Connor. She was checking his pulse, and her face was stern.

"What's going on?" I asked, temporarily proud that my voice was only shaking a little.

"Your father has been through a lot, dear," Mrs. Hearth said, glancing at me for a second. "But with Jake's help, it will work out." Jake pushed to his feet. "Sara, dear, why don't you and Lizzie finish up with the wendigo while we do this?"

I felt Jake and Sara move more than I saw it. My eyes were glued to the bloody puddle forming under Connor's head. As I watched, Mrs. Hearth turned his body over so he could breathe easier, and wouldn't choke on his own spit and blood. The sight made my heart stop. I know it didn't actually do that, but the sudden tightness in my breast made it clear that something was wrong.

Before I could start to panic, Sara's hands grabbed mine, and her face obscured Connor's. "Lizzie," she said, calm and collected as I'd ever seen her, even if her eyebrows were knitted and she looked paler than usual. "You gotta stand."

Her words just sounded like noise. I stared at her lips as they moved, saying something else, but I couldn't understand it.

"Come on, Liz," she said, and her nickname snapped me out of my staring. "You're gonna help me."

She stood, and I stood with her, never looking away from her eyes. I could hear Mrs. Hearth and Jake whispering together, but their words were too low. As Sara led me to the other side of the attic, I realized my ghosts were in an uproar. I could almost hear Eleanor snapping at someone in French, but I knew they were still at my house. I tried to send another calming wave through the threads between us, but it failed. I wasn't calm enough to calm them. The thought almost made me laugh.

Sara was saying something again. I focused and caught the

tail end of her sentence. "...Grams."

I opened my mouth and tried to ask what she'd said, but only made a strange croaking sound. It made her turn to me, though. I started to clear my throat, then felt a hand on my shoulder. Immediately, the chaos of emotions inside of me dulled from a roaring flame to a smoldering ember.

Turning my head, I saw the old hand of Mrs. Hearth. When I lifted my eyes, I saw her eyes were glowing bright yellow.

"You two finish up with the wendigo," she said, her voice as calm and warm as I'd ever heard it, and it seemed to send waves of calm through me. I felt those waves move through the threads and to my ghosts as well. Eleanor's voice in my head diminished to a whisper. "While Jake and I carry Connor downstairs and start setting the stage."

"Setting the stage?" I asked.

"Yes. The plan was to call the police, after all, and hand him over to them. With his injuries, we thought it best to make it seem like he broke in and collapsed. That way, they will bring an ambulance as well."

I swallowed, for a moment fearing the chaos of emotions roaring back to life, but it stayed dull. "He needs an ambulance?"

"Yes. The wendigo did some damage to his body that we did not foresee."

I couldn't do anything but nod. The calm waves were still dulling my emotions, and I was reaching for that numb place I'd found earlier. I was afraid the emotions of everything going on would cripple me the moment Mrs. Hearth removed her hand, and I couldn't let that happen. I had too much to do.

Mrs. Hearth turned me around with her, but I still heard Jake move behind me.

I kept my eyes on Mrs. Hearth, never looking his way. Instead,

I let Mrs. Hearth lead me to the corner where Sara was kneeling by an iron cauldron, drawing on the floor with a piece of chalk. Mrs. Hearth sat me down and patted my shoulder before she hurried away.

I listened to her feet as they rattled down the attic stairs, holding on to the numb calm as best I could. But the fear and sorrow and rage didn't ignite. They stayed calm and smoldering. There, but not so strong, I couldn't deal with them anymore.

"Her magic is really something," I said, more to say something and make sure I was really here, really awake, than to make conversation.

Sara glanced up at me with a wide grin, but her eyes were hooded and dark. "Yeah. Why do you think I used to run away to stay here every now and again? Her calming magic was the only thing that kept me from setting mom's house on fire at times."

"I thought you ran away to be with me."

Her eyes twinkled. "That too."

I smiled back, even if it was small and didn't feel completely real. "What are we doing?"

Sara returned to her drawing. "I need to get the fire sigil ready, then we put the geode into the cauldron, and I finish the sigil. When that happens, it should burn the wendigo into oblivion. Or back to the Spirit World."

"I'll get the geode."

Sara only nodded. Her tongue was poking out between her lips in concentration, and it made me warm all over.

Pushing to my feet, I walked to the altar where Sara had left the geode, making sure not to look at the small puddle of blood where Connor had been. As I reached out for the geode, I couldn't help check for the wendigo. The thread between us was still there, still as strong as it had been when I commanded it. I could feel the wendigo's rage and hunger, but even those feelings were dulled; like I was looking at them through a window. I was glad. I wasn't sure I couldn't handle the wendigo's hunger again.

Turning back to Sara, I took in the scene. She was kneeling in front of an iron cauldron the height of her torso. A black iron lid lay beside her. Beneath the cauldron was one circle with something drawn inside it that I couldn't see clearly because the cauldron stood on it. Sara was working outside a second circle, drawing the same kind of symbols that had been around the sleeping spell, but not in the same order. I compared the two circles a few times to make sure before I walked over, geode held securely with both hands.

"Now what?" I asked as I sat down in the lotus position, still holding the geode.

"Just drop it in there," Sara said and nodded at the cauldron, not lifting her eyes from her work. "I'm almost done."

I did as she said, making sure the geode didn't fall and crack open. I did not trust the candle wax and hair-bonds to keep it secure and tight, and while I might control the wendigo, I was afraid it would be able to tear free of me if released from the witch-magic. My head still hurt, although the acute pain had dulled to a rhythmic throb, and I was tired. Almost more tired than I had been after the flight to find the shaman. Not that strange, all things considered, but still. I wanted this over with, so I could rest secure in the knowledge that the wendigo wouldn't be a problem for at least a few days. I wished there was something more we could do, but I understood that we were between a rock and a hard place right now, and this was the best of two bad choices.

27

Sara stopped where I would expect her to draw one more of the symbols and lifted the lid, letting it clunk down on top of the cauldron. "Your spirit-vision on?"

"No?"

She half-smiled. "Then turn it on, this should look pretty cool."

I closed my eyes and reached for the sight. It came easier now than it had before. As the shaman said, the power wanted to be used, and it seemed like a muscle. The more I used it, the easier it was. It still took almost a minute before I opened my eyes again, however, and when I did, Sara stared into nothing, seeming far away.

"You ok?" I asked, and she jumped, blinking to bring me into focus.

"Yeah. Just thinking. Ready?"

I nodded, and she drew the last sign.

Instantly, a fire roared up around the cauldron. I pushed back, gasping in surprise as the heat hit me in the face. For a moment, a primal part of me wanted to run, but I pushed it down and took in the fire.

It wasn't really there, and I could see that now that I was over the first shock. It licked and moved and devoured like normal fire, but it was blueish white, and I could see Sara on the other side of it, her glowing yellow eyes reflecting the fire.

"Wow," I mumbled.

Sara gave a real smirk. "Right?"

I was about to say something else when the thread binding me to the wendigo moved. It pulled, and almost pulling me into the fire with it. I pushed back, fighting to stay where I was as the heat of the fire almost touched my face. I heard Sara say my name as the heat spread from my face and down my neck, over my back, and into my chest. It was too hot. It burned. I gasped for breath and felt the heat soar down my windpipe, flashing through my lungs and burning them like rice paper. Hands touched me, and I tried to struggle free, the touch just making the feeling of fire hotter. I wanted to scream, but there was only fire inside me, only pain. I was burning from the inside out!

Then it was over. Just as fast as the pull had happened, it disappeared. My skin and lungs felt like cool ashes, and I stared at the white flames as the thread between me and the wendigo slackened, then hung limp. There was nothing on the other end. The wendigo was gone.

28

After making sure I was ok, Sara returned her attention to the cauldron.

"Did you hear a crack?" she asked as she walked around it.

"A crack? No, can't say I did," I answered, staying where I was. My whole body felt light, but I didn't quite trust it.

Sara muttered something under her breath before she reached for an iron rod that stood leaning against the wall. Using the hook at its end, she lifted the lid off the cauldron and looked inside. I couldn't help leaning forward to see as well.

"Careful," she said, freezing me in mid-lean. "Don't cross the circle, and don't touch the flames."

I mock-scowled at her. "I figured as much."

"Feeling secure in your knowledge of the magical world?"

"Far from it! Which is why I won't cross any lines drawn by a witch. Ever!"

Sara grinned. "Good."

She turned her eyes back to the cauldron, and I did as well. Inside, the geode lay cracked open. There was no sign of the hair-threads Sara had used to tie it in place, and the candle-wax had melted to a small puddle at the bottom.

Sara let out an audible breath.

"What does that mean?" I asked.

"It means the wendigo has left the building," she answered as she lowered the lid back onto the cauldron. "Which means we have to get our asses downstairs."

Putting the rod back against the wall, she smudged one of the signs framing the circle with her foot. The moment it was destroyed, the fire within the circle disappeared. One moment, it was roaring along merrily, the next it was just gone.

I stayed where I was, watching as Sara lifted the cauldron with a grunt and rested it against her hip. Standing like that, she used her foot to drag an X through the circle, her fluffy socks smudging the lines. I could almost see the magic escaping through the breaks and blinked off my spirit-vision. It took me a few seconds to focus back on the real world; my eyes were so tired.

Sara put the cauldron back down and stretched her arms into the air.

"You back?" she asked.

"Yes. Sorry."

"Nothing to say sorry for. It's been a long day. C'mon." I climbed to my feet, and we walked side by side to the attic-door. "Usually, I don't like leaving tools of the craft lying around," Sara was saying. "One never knows what they can conjure up, but I don't have time to clean everything right now."

She scowled around the attic as if it was the room's fault before she opened the door and waved me through.

"Conjure up?" I asked. "Can magic just happen on its own?"

"Yeah," Sara said as she closed the door behind her, but instead of following me down the stairs, she turned back to the door. I couldn't see what she was doing past her body, but I heard her mutter in the same strange language as while we cast the searching spell earlier that morning. Then the lock clicked.

She turned to me and started herding me down the stairs as she continued. "Like with science, magical energy has to go somewhere. If we're not careful, it'll go somewhere it's not supposed to."

"Like?"

She didn't answer as we left the stairs, and I watched as she locked the almost hidden door, put the key in the flowerpot, then pulled the pot in front of the door. I had all but given up on her answering and wouldn't push her, when she turned to me. Her eyes were dark and serious.

"Depends on where the magical energy was gathering. Sometimes, it'll create random effects like draining a phone battery that passes through it or messing with other electrical things. Or, if you're really unlucky, it can form into a sentient being."

I stared at her, unsure of what to say. Finally, I found something: "So what about all the magic upstairs? Can that morph into a being we have to deal with when we go back up there?"

Sara linked her arm with mine and started leading me downstairs. "No. We always make sure to cleanse the space between castings. We make sure there's no residual magic hanging around, waiting for a chance to mess with us." She gave a half-grin that didn't reach her eyes. "Even if we leave the things up there as they are for a few days, nothing'll happen. All the circles have been broken, the magic released back into the world, and there's no spirits or magical objects hanging around, waiting. It would be a lot scarier if we didn't deal with the wendigo beforehand."

I nodded. There was still a lot I wanted to know about the magical world, but I was too tired to think up a good question right now. And it wasn't like we had the time anyway.

The moment we stepped into view of the ground floor, Mrs. Hearth nodded and lifted the phone. As she dialed up the police, Jake led us into the living room as he explained what we would say when the police arrived.

I wasn't listening. My eyes had found Connor lying in the hallway, sprawled on his side, put in a position where he wouldn't drown on his own spit. Someone had poured water all over him and then splattered it across the hallway floor, making it look like he'd pulled it with him as he entered from the outside.

Connor was still missing his shoe, and I wondered where it was. If it lay in the back of Mrs. Hearth's car, or if it was still at the caves, or somewhere else. Maybe he'd lost it in the woods as he ran from here last night?

"Lizzie?" Jake's voice made me return my attention to him. "Are you listening?"

"No," I sighed. "Sorry."

Jake only nodded and started from the top. I let Sara lower me onto the couch as he spoke, and it wasn't hard to feign the exhausted shock he wanted me to show the police. It wasn't hard at all.

29

Everything after that was kind of a blur. I was exhausted in both body and mind, and I felt the worry from my ghosts. I knew they wanted to be here with me, wanted to support me, but that they stayed away as I had asked, even if it brought them sorrow. Their feelings on top of my own were distracting.

I hardly noticed when the paramedics arrived, leaving Mrs. Hearth to deal with them. I heard her words, but it felt like I couldn't focus on the people talking.

"He was agitated when he arrived?" A woman's voice asked.

"Yes," Mrs. Hearth answered. "He raved about I don't even know what."

"And you think he didn't recognize you?"

"He recognized Lizzie."

"Who's that?"

I zoned out as Mrs. Hearth explained our situation and the lie we'd all agreed on.

I had fallen into a daze when Sara's voice woke me up again. "What're you doing?"

My eyes jumped to the hallway, where the paramedics were maneuvering their stretcher toward the door. Connor lay on it; his face turned toward us. It was too pale, which only made the blood on his lips and around his nose and eyes stand out even more.

I let out a soundless noise and turned away. Jake was behind me and instantly wrapped his arms around me, holding me and letting me hide against his chest. A small part of me was embarrassed for the reaction and seeking comfort from a man I hardly knew, while another was thankful for his comfort.

Voices were talking back and forth, but I forced myself not to listen, instead focusing on Jake's heartbeat and the sound of my own breathing. I didn't look up before someone touched my shoulder.

I had to blink back tears, but even before I could see clearly, I recognized Mrs. Hearth. She was saying something. I could see her lips moving, but her voice was garbled.

Shaking my head, I forced myself to focus. "Sorry, what did you say?"

Mrs. Hearth gave a small sigh that somehow held the worry and sorrow of a whole generation. "The police are here. The detectives we told you about?"

"Oh," I said. "What about Connor?"

"You don't call him dad or father?" Someone asked from behind Mrs. Hearth.

"Seriously?" Sara asked, her voice hard and venomous.

"It was just a question," the same voice answered, but it didn't sound apologetic.

I shook my head again, trying to wake up. "No," I answered, trying to look past Mrs. Hearth and Sara, who both stood in front of me, like a shield. Jake's arm was still around my shoulder. "I haven't called him that for a week or so."

"Only a week?"

"Yes, until then, I tried to forget that he existed, to be honest."

Mrs. Hearth turned at my yawn. "I will make some coffee," she said, squeezing my shoulder once before she walked away, finally letting me see the owner of the voice.

Two new people stood in the hallway. A tall man with a thin face and body, and an almost as tall woman with twice as broad shoulders. They were both dressed in a shirt and dark jeans, the woman was without makeup and her hair pulled into a messy ponytail. The man still had pillow-streaks on his cheek. They must have been woken up and rushed here.

The woman was the first to move. She was about to walk into the living room but stopped at Sara's angry voice. "We don't wear shoes inside here."

The woman and man glanced at each other, but both pushed out of their shoes before entering the living room. That little show of dominance from Sara put me strangely at ease. Like we were taking control of our own world again. I hadn't had that feeling in a while, I realized.

"My name is Melania Bell," the woman said, reaching out her hand. I shook it, before turning toward the man. He shook my hand and introduced himself as Henrik Vandom. They shook hands with Jake and Sara as well, not saying more than their names again and again.

"You prefer we call you Lizzie?" Vandom asked as he sunk into one of the chairs across from me.

I opened my mouth to answer, but I wasn't sure what I was going to say. I'd hated that name just yesterday, getting sick from hearing it, but during this day, it had somehow gotten less dangerous. I hadn't even realized that before now. That by doing the things I had done in the last twenty-four hours, I had started taking my name back.

"Yes," I said in a rush. "Sorry, it's been a long night."

"I can believe that!" Bell said. "When did you come home? Sometime after nine, I'd say."

"At one," Jake answered. "Feels like we were just in bed when... Connor came."

"I can imagine," Bell said, her eyes jumping between me, Jake, and Sara. "I'm sorry if I seem confused, but Jake is your boyfriend, Sara?"

"Yeah," Sara said from my right side. Her arm and leg were both flushed against mine, her warmth mixing with mine and keeping me awake. Jake's arm still lay across my neck, his fingers on Sara's shoulder.

"So why did you not go with him on this trip today? And where did you go?" the last she directed at me.

"She didn't go because my daughter and granddaughter got in a bit of a fight two days ago, and we wanted to clear that up. Without Jake and Lizzie here to antagonize her," Mrs. Hearth said as she entered the living room with a tray of cups and cans. The smell of coffee wafted around us, invigorating in its own power.

"Why not?"

"Because we were the cause of the discussion," Jake answered.

"Why?"

"Is that relevant somehow?"

"No, I'm just way too interested in gossip," Bell gave a small chuckle before thanking Mrs. Hearth for the cup of coffee she was offered.

"You didn't answer her question," Vandom said after accepting his own coffee. "Where did you go?"

"Potlotek Nation," Jake said.

"What were you doing there?"

"Looking for a shaman."

Bell almost choked on her coffee.

"Whatever for?" Vandom asked as he banged his partner on the back. He never took his eyes off me.

"Because I wanted to talk to him," I answered, speaking up for the first time since introducing myself. "After mom died... I've been curious about my heritage, and I figured maybe they knew something."

Vandom and Bell exchanged a glance, Bell still coughing a little. That look said a lot, but I didn't know what. Finally, Vandom cleared his throat and asked about tonight.

We gave him the same story we'd given the paramedics. That Connor had come on the door, banging and yelling for Mrs. Hearth to open. That he mumbled something when she let him in, seeming almost confused at his surroundings, until he saw me. At that, he started rambling and moved forward, but collapsed where the paramedics found him.

The questions moved to my relationship with Connor and his new family. I was honest. What was it they said on crime-shows? Be true as far as possible; it will make the lies more believable?

What about the last time we saw him? What did he want then? He wanted to talk about the house, but Mrs. Hearth chased him out when he began yelling. Yes, we had noticed his car in my driveway. No, we hadn't given it much thought. Other things were more pressing.

The questions just kept coming and coming. It was clear that Vandom didn't like that we were all in the living room and answering around each other, but when he asked to speak to me alone, Jake asked pretty pointedly if I was a suspect in Connor's disappearance. Considering we'd found him again, I couldn't be, but I saw in the set of Vandom's jaw that he thought I'd done something, even if he couldn't put his finger on what.

We'd started on our second pot of coffee when the questions finally went somewhere else.

"Do you know this man?" Bell asked, handing me a photo.

A man barely older than me smiled up at me. I blinked, and the picture shimmered in front of me. Overlapping the smiling man, I saw the same face covered in blood, head busted open.

My stomach churned, and I gasped for air. At the last moment, I turned the gasp into a yawn, fighting not to curl around my moving stomach. The coffee seemed to burn its way up my throat as I handed the picture to Sara.

"No," I said when my pretend yawn was over. My voice was still a little tight from my battle with my stomach, but the detectives didn't seem to notice. "Who is he?"

"Philip Hammond," Bell answered as she took the picture back. "He also went missing a few days ago."

Jake's arm jumped a little. "That's the man they found yesterday, wasn't it? He was dead?" All eyes turned to him, and he shrugged. "I remember the name from the news."

"Oh," I said, my churning stomach going stone cold. That was why I'd seen his face before. It was the man Connor ate. "I'm sorry," I said and pushed to my feet.

I heard someone say my name, but I was running for the kitchen, not looking back.

My hands were barely on the counter when I flung myself forward and puked in the sink. The bitter taste of coffee for a second turned to the memory of blood, and I retched again, the content of my stomach burning into my eyes.

Someone touched my back, and I spun around, tears streaming and mouth panting.

"It's ok," Sara said. "It's been a long day. We'll ask them to leave and come back tomorrow."

I shook my head and reached for the paper towels. Sara stepped out of the way so I could wash my mouth. When I looked up from the sink again, she was holding a dry piece of bread. I started to turn away, but she pushed the bread in my face.

"The rest of us have eaten a cookie or two. You've drunk two cups of coffee on an empty stomach. No wonder your body rebelled."

I accepted the piece and forced down a bite. The bread was so far from the consistency of flesh as one could come, so while I thought about Connor eating a man partly alive, I didn't get the dream memory of the meal. It almost made me cry with relief.

Sara narrowed her eyes. "Or wasn't it the coffee?"

I glanced toward the closed door but didn't dare speak, so I shook my head in silent answer.

Sara grimaced before she nodded and wrapped her arms around me, hugging me tight for a second before she led me back into the living room. I forced down another piece of the bread.

"Sorry," I said. "I haven't eaten much today, and the coffee."

Bell lifted her hands and tipped her head in an ''I understand''-gesture. "And it's been a long night for you. No body would be too happy about that. At least mine isn't!"

I gave half a smile and forced down another bite of the bread. My stomach had calmed, but I could still see Philip Hammond's bloody face every time I blinked.

"He was dead, wasn't he?" I asked after another bite. "This Philip? You think he was somehow connected to Connor?"

Bell and Vandom glanced at each other before Vandom shrugged. "We're holding every possibility open. There's been a lot of disappearances this last week, which is surprising in a small town like Sky Harbour. I don't even remember the last time a detective had to come here."

"Must be something in the air or the water," I said around another bite. It was turning to dust in my mouth, but it was a good excuse to not focus on the detectives.

"Maybe," Vandom answered.

"How many are missing?" Jake asked.

"Almost a hundred at this time, and that's just in Sky Harbour."

I swallowed the piece of bread wrong and coughed and spluttered. Sara pounded on my back.

"That many?" I wheezed when the bite was down the right pipe. "But didn't the news say most turned up again? Why haven't we heard anything about this?"

"We've been trying to avoid a panic," Bell said. "But after Philip turned up... tomorrow, the local paper and news will issue a curfew until this is solved. Most of the disappearances seem to happen at night, so just lock your door and don't open it for anyone, even someone you know." She glanced toward the hallway and the spot where we'd placed Connor.

I only nodded, not sure what else to say. It must be because of the Rift and the creatures spilling into our world. Considering that, it was a wonder the whole town hadn't been erased. It left me with a foul taste in my mouth. All that blood was on my hands.

Bell and Vandom came with a few more questions before finally saying they were done. The bread lay heavy in my stomach by then, but I hadn't drunk any more coffee.

We walked the detectives to the door as the clock on the mantelpiece chimed four times. The tolls making both Jake and me slump with exhaustion, and it was a relief when we could finally lock the door behind the detectives.

Instantly, I tugged at the threads leading to my ghosts. They appeared before I'd turned away from the door, making me jump and stumble from exhaustion. Eleanor apologized in French, but I only shook my head and turned to the twins.

"Please follow the two detectives and listen to what they say about us." I turned to the other ghosts as the twins jogged past me and right through the front door. "Can you please scan the neighborhood for any witches? Just do one quick look, and at least two-and-two together, then get back here."

"Will you sleep?" Eleanor asked, her eyes narrowed and face set in an annoyed frown I recognized from mom when I'd stayed up far too long. I nodded and let Sara tug me toward the stairs. I was too tired to fight back, and hardly even felt the ghosts move away from me. I wasn't even completely there when I fell into bed.

To be continued...

Afterword

I guess there's a lot of people I can thank for this book in some way or another.

I know I need to thank my partner. I owe them everything. Both for my falling in love with writing, but also for them standing by my side through something no couple at our age should have to live through.

Thank you for staying with me, you're my hero, and I hope you know it.

I also need to thank my beta readers. Evelyn, Anniken, Courney, and Kristina. Your feedback was invaluable, and I wouldn't have had the guts to publish if not for your help. Not to mention this book would be something completely different without you, and I'm so grateful it turned out the way it did! Thank you so, so much!

Thank you to Solstice for helping me with the French part! It would have been a mess of Google Translate, if not for you.

Thank you to Anna Mia for Gudrun. This character wouldn't have excisted without you, and I'm so glad it does!

And thank you so much to A. J. Wolf for the cover!

Lastly, a comment on magical creatures.

Wendigos are originally a mythological man-eating creature

or evil spirit from the folklore of the First Nations Algonquian tribes from Canada. The wendigo you read about in this book, is adopted and changed to fit my story, so do not take my wendigo as fact.

I also have to say that I am not of First Nation or Native American. My shamans are not realistic representative of the shamans of this culture.

About the Author

Kima Blaze lives in along the fjords of Norway, with her partner and lover, and their dog.

Kima came late to the writing game, discovering it in her early twenties when sickness took hold of her life. Her partner, who had been writing their entire life, suggested Kima write down her frustration. She hasn't stopped writing since.

CURSE OF A NAME is her first published work.

You can connect with me on:

https://twitter.com/KimaBlaze

Subscribe to my newsletter:

https://landing.mailerlite.com/webforms/landing/u6f9x4

Also by Kima Blaze

A RIFT IN THE VEIL–series
  Curse of a Name
  Reflections
  The Curse of Sight

Curse of a Name

After returning to her childhood home to care for her Alzheimers sick mother, Elizabeth ''Lizzie'' Key starts having nightmares of women dying through history. All of them with her name. While trying to help her violent mother and at the same time keep her own sanity, Lizzie can't be sure if her dreams and her mother's ramblings are in truth a warning, or if she herself is getting sick.

But she can't shake the feeling that many of her family's ghosts are real, and some of them are more bloodthirsty than others.

Reflections

Witches have two jobs:

One: make sure the Veil stays strong and in place.

Two: deal with ghosts or spirits that get through the Veil.

It's an easy job. The biggest baddies don't get through, and the ghosts that start making trouble aren't even worth worrying about. Any witch with awakened powers can take care of them.

So when girls start going missing, Sara Hearth realizes there's a spirit of some kind involved. She expects an easy fix but soon learns that this spirit is something new, something powerful, and she has no idea how to fight it or save the girls.

Sara is lucky, but will it be enough?

————————————————————————————

This story is set between CURSE OF A NAME and THE CURSE OF SIGHT.

It can be read as a stand-alone.

WARNING: This book contains spoilers for CURSE OF A NAME.

The Curse of Sight

It's been a week of nightmares.

In her dreams, Lizzie runs through grey worlds and hunts in the dark, driven by a bloodlust that isn't her own.

Awake, she is haunted by ghosts from both past and present. Some are the ghosts of family members that she has sworn to help. Others are the ghosts of feelings and decisions not made.

It's been a week since her life changed forever. A week since she died and came back.

But in breaking free of death, Lizzie broke something else. She tore the Veil keeping humans safe, allowing monsters and spirits to flood our world.

It's been a week since she awoke as a shaman.

And as a shaman, it's Lizzie's job to fix what she broke.

www.ingramcontent.com/pod-product-compliance
Lightning Source LLC
Chambersburg PA
CBHW020339160726
47992CB00004B/1882